American

HEROES

AGAINST ALL ODDS

Jackie
Merritt

Black Creek Ranch

Silhouette Books

Published by Silhouette Books

America's Publisher of Contemporary Romance

W9-BEK-958

If you purchased this book without a cover you should be aware
that this book is stolen property. It was reported as "unsold and
destroyed" to the publisher, and neither the author nor the
publisher has received any payment for this "stripped book."

SILHOUETTE BOOKS
300 East 42nd St.,
New York, N. Y. 10017

ISBN 0-373-82248-0

BLACK CREEK RANCH

Copyright © 1992 by Carolyn Joyner

All rights reserved. Except for use in any review, the reproduction
or utilization of this work in whole or in part in any form by any
electronic, mechanical or other means, now known or hereafter
invented, including xerography, photocopying and recording, or in
any information storage or retrieval system, is forbidden without
the written permission of the editorial office, Silhouette Books,
300 East 42nd Street, New York, NY 10017 U.S.A.

All characters in this book have no existence outside the imagination of
the author and have no relation whatsoever to anyone bearing the same
name or names. They are not even distantly inspired by any individual
known or unknown to the author, and all incidents are pure invention.

This edition published by arrangement with Harlequin Books S.A.

® and TM are trademarks of Harlequin Books S.A., used under license.
Trademarks indicated with ® are registered in the United States Patent
and Trademark Office, the Canadian Trade Marks Office and in other
countries.

Visit Silhouette at www.eHarlequin.com

Printed in U.S.A.

About the Author

Jackie Merritt and her husband have settled once more in the Southwest after traveling around the West and Northwest for a while—Jackie wanted to soak up the atmosphere and find new locales and inspirations for her appealing Western stories.

An accountant for many years, Jackie has happily traded numbers for words. Next to family, books are her greatest joy. She started writing in 1987, and her efforts paid off in 1988 with the publication of her first novel. When she's not writing or enjoying a good book, Jackie dabbles in watercolor painting and likes playing the piano.

Books by Jackie Merritt

Dear Reader,

When I was notified that *Black Creek Ranch* was going to be reissued, I tried to recall what prompted that particular story. I found the story again, and reread some of the book. I like Drew, the heroine—she's strong, independent and a helicopter pilot—and Nick, the hero, who has a heartbreaking past to overcome. I even like Drew's overbearing, chauvinistic brothers. And it's not exaggerating at all to say that Wyoming is one of my favorite states.

So, with all of those "likes," where on earth did the story come from? Beats me. Maybe after forty-four books an author's mind clouds on some details. Was I in Wyoming in 1992, and did I meet a female copter pilot? I don't think so, and as far as I can remember, to this day, every pilot I know—fixed-wing or chopper—is male.

Setting a book in Wyoming is not unusual for me, so I won't even look for a specific reason for that. But the LeBeau family and Nick Orion? They *are* unusual and must have been conjured up from the depths of my imagination.

At any rate, it's a darned good story!

Jackie Merritt

Please address questions and book requests to:
Silhouette Reader Service
U.S.: 3010 Walden Ave., P.O. Box 1325, Buffalo, NY 14269
Canadian: P.O. Box 609, Fort Erie, Ont. L2A 5X3

One

The four-seat copter was well on its way before Nick Orion leaned forward and took notice of his—woman?—pilot. Now he sat back with a frown while a vague memory took shape: George Hollister, his right-hand man, had mentioned a different pilot for today's flight.

But had George indicated a lady pilot?

Nick honestly couldn't remember. He'd been relying on George more and more of late—that was the one thing he knew with every certainty.

The person at the controls was definitely female, which Nick knew would have been instantly obvious had he bothered to pull himself out of the fog of numbers and decisions crowding his thoughts long enough for a civil hello.

He rubbed his jaw thoughtfully. He had nothing against women, in general, or women pilots, specifically. But the fact that he could board his helicopter without seeing the pilot, at all, was disconcerting. He knew he'd been stretching himself—and George—for a long time. Three or four other people in the company were working themselves into an early grave, too. Orion, Inc. was a demanding mistress, and he and some very loyal staff members were succumbing to its allure without so much as a whisper of protest.

Time was money. That was why he used a helicopter to visit the company's various development sites, instead of a car. There were four projects locked into the sales program at present, all within a two-hundred-mile radius of Laramie, Wyoming. There were two others in the making, one of which Nick felt a particular fondness for, a scenic ranch that boasted an especially appealing ribbon of water called Black Creek.

In fact...

Puzzled at the direction they were traveling, Nick leaned forward and tapped the pilot on the shoulder. "Black Creek Ranch isn't on my agenda today," he said loudly enough to be heard above the copter's noise. "Why are we heading southwest?"

Drew gave the man behind her a quick glance. "I think it's time I introduced myself, Mr. Orion. I'm Drew LeBeau."

Nick caught a glimpse of an extremely pretty mouth. Much of the woman's face was concealed by mirrored sunglasses. Her hair was honey blond and arranged in a short, no-nonsense style that seemed attractive to Nick. All in all, he had an impression of pleasing femaleness in his pilot.

But her name surprised him. He'd been negotiating with the LeBeau brothers, Judd and Simon, to purchase the LeBeau family's Black Creek Ranch, and they had

"Lady, if you were a man..."

Nick yelled.

Watching Nick storm around, Drew took note of the man's excellent physique, his broad shoulders, his lean hips, his long legs. He was wearing jeans, black cowboy boots and a white shirt. He must have been well over six feet tall.

"Just how in the hell are we going to get out of here?" His hard blue eyes narrowed on her. "Got any suggestions?" he said angrily.

"Look," Drew said with a scowl, "I'm sorry. I never intended to put you in jeopardy."

"It will be days before anyone figures out we're stranded here, Drew."

"Days?" Drew swallowed hard. Days out here in the middle of nowhere with this loathsome individual? Well, at least they wouldn't starve, and they did have a roof over their heads. And eventually someone would come along—right?

Wyoming
State Facts

Nickname: The Equality State

Date Entered Union: July 10, 1890
(the 44th state)

Motto: Equal rights

Wyoming Men: Jackson Pollock, *painter*
Alan K. Simpson, *senator*
Chief Washakie, *chief of the Shoshone*
James G. Watt, *former U.S. secretary of the Interior*

Song: "Wyoming," words by Charles E. Winter, music by G. E. Knapp

Flower: Indian paintbrush

Bird: Western meadowlark

Fun Facts: Wyoming was the first state to give women the right to vote.

Cody, Wyoming, is named after William "Buffalo Bill" Cody.

told him their sister was a little reluctant to sell. They had also said that Drew was a pilot for the U.S. Forest Service, but how in heck had she gotten into the Orion company's helicopter?

"I don't think I understand," he said with a truly perplexed frown.

Drew had been wondering about Orion's lack of communication. He'd seemed so absorbed, and she had waited for him to speak first, not wanting to interrupt his circumspection. "Most of the copter pilots in the area are good friends, Mr. Orion. When your usual driver, Will Torgeson—" Drew pronounced "driver" with a touch of humor "—called me this morning and asked if I would handle this flight for him, I saw it as a good opportunity for you and I to meet."

"Why couldn't Will do it?"

"He said something about a minor emergency. I'm sure he cleared our arrangement with someone in your organization."

"Hollister," Nick said in an undertone, recalling again that George had made reference to a different pilot.

"Pardon?"

"Nothing important." It suddenly occurred to Nick that Drew LeBeau wanting to meet him could be a good sign that she was relenting on the sale of the ranch.

Still, Black Creek wasn't on his tightly planned agenda for today, and he'd already flown over the ranch on numerous occasions.

"Tell me why you're heading for Black Creek," he said.

"It's just a small detour," Drew replied over her shoulder. "Do you mind?"

"Not if there's a good reason. I've already seen the place from the air several times."

"Seeing the place from the air" wasn't all that Drew was hoping for. If Orion agreed, she wanted to set down. Drew still couldn't believe her brothers were seriously considering selling the LeBeau family ranch to a land developer. Their majority vote was a mite overwhelming, so she'd decided to circumvent Judd and Simon and speak to Orion herself about his plans for the ranch.

All she wanted was an hour of Orion's uninterrupted attention. And what better, more influencing place to talk about the ranch than the LeBeau land itself? This morning's phone call from Will Torgeson had created an opportunity she hadn't been able to pass up.

Drew took a rather nervous breath. Visualizing herself presenting an unscheduled stop to Nick Orion had been much easier than its reality. For one thing, Orion was an intimidating man, which she hadn't expected. He was also very good-looking—which shouldn't matter, but seemed to.

She knew a few facts about him, how he'd started a land-development company with little or nothing a few years back and had woven it into a successful, respected firm. He wasn't married, nor, to her knowledge, ever had been. If rumor had any foundation, he was a workaholic, a man who didn't waste precious time on frivolous pastimes.

She believed it now, just from the stern lines in the man's handsome face.

His good looks did a few predictable things to her libido, but weren't assets as far as the situation went. Gathering her courage, Drew glanced back at him again. "Mr. Orion, I'd like to set down."

"At the ranch? What for?"

Drew had to think about the question. What, really, was she hoping to accomplish? Orion was a developer, a businessman, and not apt to be influenced by an emotional appeal to keep the land intact. Why else would he buy it, if not for profit?

Her spirits dropped a notch. She and Judd and Simon had recently had several heated discussions on the ranch, but it wasn't the idea of selling that had been bothering her so much—it was selling to a developer, a man who probably was planning to rip the land into little pieces and offer it to any greenhorn with the price in his jeans.

She had gotten a bit melodramatic on the subject, Drew realized. But they were nearly over the ranch, and if Orion didn't object to setting down, maybe he wouldn't object to listening to her reasons for disliking the prospect of selling to a serious developer. Maybe he would consider breaking the ranch only a few times, like cutting it into quarters and selling to four prospective ranchers. Something like that was floating around in the back of her mind, Drew knew, although she didn't want to state her rather nebulous case with her back to the man.

She started to say so when Orion leaned forward again. "I'd welcome the chance for us to talk, Drew, but I don't have the time today. My schedule is really tight. We could set up a meeting for tomorrow, and..."

Drew listened to the voice behind her with a sinking sensation. Orion *was* objecting to a stop at the ranch, rather adamantly, in fact, and she was hardly in a position to argue with him about it.

She heaved a private sigh of defeat. Her idea probably wouldn't have changed anything, anyway.

The engine suddenly emitted a strange cough, a questionable hesitation in performance. Drew's thoughts jumped from her own personal distress to the machine she was flying. "I don't like the sound of the engine," she said over her shoulder.

"What's wrong?"

"Could be a clog in a fuel line." She felt Orion practically climbing over the seat to see the dials on the console.

"The oil pressure is dropping," he exclaimed.

Drew had already taken note of the oil-pressure gauge, and while the drop wasn't severe, it wasn't something to overlook. The engine sputtered again. Drew looked out the window, checking for a clearing. The immediate area was mountainous, and dense with trees.

Nick, too, turned his attention to the terrain below. If a mechanical problem brought them down out here, they'd be miles from a telephone. The copter didn't have a radio, either, which had come up for discussion several times. He'd bought the bird from a rancher who'd gone on to a newer and better equipped model, and he should have had a radio installed right away. Nick grumbled under his breath. If they landed out here, they'd be stranded a hundred miles from Laramie with no way to contact anyone and the day's detailed schedule would go down the drain.

Drew was all business now. "We're nearly to the ranch. I'm going to put her down there and check the fuel line."

"Do you know what to do?"

For the first time in their brief acquaintance, Drew felt some annoyance with her passenger, suspecting that Orion wouldn't have asked a male pilot if he knew what to do with a clogged fuel line. "Yes, I know what to do," she said rather curtly.

Nick sent her a sharp look. He knew something about engines, in general, but he wasn't a pilot or an expert on helicopters. They were going to set down at Black Creek, against his earlier objections, and was Drew LeBeau capable of manipulating a situation to get something she wanted?

Why in hell had she wanted him out here, anyway? They should already be landing at the first site on his list, not hovering over the LeBeaus' Black Creek Ranch! And a mechanical problem on lower, more populated ground would be a heck of a lot easier to deal with than it would be in these mountains.

"Don't land," he said brusquely.

Startled, Drew shot Orion a disbelieving glance. "I don't think we have a choice."

"The engine sounds fine now. Turn the bird around and head back."

"Mr. Orion..."

"Do as I say!"

Drew wavered for a moment. This was his helicopter, but if he were a pilot, *he'd* be at the controls, not her! It would only take twenty, thirty minutes, maybe less, to blow out the fuel lines.

The decision was wrested out of her hands by another sputtering of the engine. "Sorry," she said firmly. "I'm setting down."

Nick's stomach had started acting up. He'd been having trouble with indigestion, anyway, and contemplating a landing in the middle of nowhere seemed to have delivered a spurt of burning acid right between his pectorals. Grimacing, he tenderly fingered the spot, then dug a roll of antacid tablets out of his vest pocket and ate two of them.

The engine was responding erratically, which was breaking the rhythm of the rotors. "Make sure your safety belt is secure," Drew called out.

"Great," Nick muttered, and tested the tautness of the belt clamping him to the seat. He studied the ground through the Plexiglas on his left and recognized some features of Black Creek Ranch. Trees and rocks flashed beneath the copter. Without Drew LeBeau manipulating his flight schedule, they would be landing at one of the relatively busy development sites. Instead, they were going to set down on the heart of an uninhabited cattle ranch. The LeBeaus hadn't lived in the place in years, and to Nick's knowledge, neighbors were few and far between.

Drew was concentrating on landing the bird, having already mentally picked a level spot. Black Creek Ranch was not located on the flats. Rather, its two thousand acres encompassed some very rugged country in south-central Wyoming. The Rockies and the Continental Divide were part of the general area. Blackhall Mountain, Bridger Peak and Snowy Range Pass all exceeded ten thousand feet, but they were surpassed by Medicine Bow Peak, a twelve-thousand-foot beauty. The scenery was breathtaking, both on and off the ranch.

Landing wasn't going to be a simple matter, Drew realized uneasily, as the copter swept over the old ranch house nearly close enough to reach out and touch its shake roof. The powerful windstorm the area had suffered three nights before had inflicted a lot of damage. Limbs and branches from the dense pine-and-fir forest were strewn all over the place, even in the small clearing she had planned on using for a helipad.

It flitted through Drew's mind that a landing under these circumstances was going to be tricky business. But the next nearest clearing, a grassy plateau that had been the LeBeaus' main grazing area at one time, was quite some distance away, and the engine was dying a slow but certain death. Without the storm, she'd have brought the bird down with the gentle thrust of a dropping feather. Now...?

"Damn," she mumbled as she swung the copter sharply to the right to avoid a massive, obtrusive branch. It was impossible to avoid so much debris, she realized as the rotors struck another branch. A cutting whine, indicating damage to the rotors, jangled her nerves.

Drew worked the controls with her every sense attuned to the emergency. Choices had suddenly disappeared. Adrenaline pumped through her system hard and fast. She'd made only one other forced landing in her flying career and it had been under much better conditions. The ground was littered with unanchored fallen brush and the rotors were stirring it up into a nearly blinding turmoil.

Nick hadn't missed the altered rhythm of the rotors. He swallowed the discomfiting lump that had suddenly appeared in his throat. He wasn't a white-knuckle flyer, but a simple problem with the fuel system had evolved into dangerous business. The copter had clipped something, a tree or a branch, and the machine was teetering, swaying within a maelstrom of flying debris.

And then, rather abruptly, he felt solid ground beneath the skids. His pulse was running wild and he wiped his mouth with the back of his hand, feeling a tremendous relief in his gut.

Drew's hands were trembling, an aftereffect of so much tension. She cut the engine and the wheezing rotors began to slow down. They were on the ground and safe, but it had been touch and go for a few breath-stealing moments.

Nick unsnapped his safety belt and then just sat there. Everything seemed almost lethally quiet without the engine and rotors operating. He couldn't believe that he was out here at all, let alone with the copter disabled.

At one time he'd lived with anger as a constant companion. Learning how to channel such a strong destructive emotion into productivity had taken a while, but he'd managed to do it. Now, the anger burned again, or something very close to it.

His voice was hoarse with barely contained fury. "This is a helluva mess you got us into."

"What?" Stunned, Drew tried to twist in the seat to see her passenger. "It's hardly my fault your helicopter isn't in better condition. For your information, *I* got us *out* of a mess!"

"I'm here because I want to be? *I* told you to bring me out here?"

Drew turned around, facing front again, abruptly. He was right. Orion wouldn't be out here without her creative maneuvering of his schedule. But she had just saved his arrogant butt, and it wouldn't hurt him to acknowledge it!

Still, there was no question that they were stuck out here. One or more of the rotors had gotten nicked, putting it out of sync. They didn't dare risk a takeoff until it was checked and repaired, and that was only one of the things Drew knew that she couldn't do without the right tools. She suddenly felt awful, guilty as sin and weak with regret. Orion had a right to be ticked off. Not that the clogged fuel line had been her fault, but if she had stayed with his schedule, they would be on lower ground and closer to assistance.

Caught by her seat belt, Drew released it with shaking hands. Then, finally, she was able to turn around and give Nick Orion a look at her guilty face. In fact, she took off her mirrored glasses to give him a really good look. "I'm terribly sorry," she said huskily.

Nick stared. She was a pretty woman, around thirty, he estimated. No cream puff, although that silky blond hair was tempting enough for any man. She had tiny lines at the corners of her compelling green eyes, as though she smiled and laughed a lot. She wasn't smiling now.

He couldn't be generous, not when he knew how stranded they were. No radio, no telephone, no neighbors. And worse, did anyone know Drew had planned to take them out here?

Nick stared at her, his vivid blue eyes glittering dangerously. Drew's regret began receding. Orion was furious and not even attempting to pretend otherwise, and her own spirit always rebelled at unreasonable condemnation. She had brought them down safely against tremendous odds. Didn't the man realize that?

But Orion's anger wasn't her most pressing problem right now. No one knew where they were, and this bird wasn't going to fly again until its rotor blades were repaired. She would inspect them, of course, but she already knew they'd been damaged.

Drew felt like an idiot. Her plan had seemed so logical when she'd thought of it during Will Torgeson's call this morning. She'd visualized herself and Orion standing on the old ranch house's back porch, looking off at the incredible forever view, and him listening to how crass the destruction of such beauty would be. Even so, she had already decided it would do little good before the damned engine started missing.

"Suppose you tell me what this is all about," Nick demanded. This nitwit had nearly gotten him killed, and for what? "Was there really a problem with the fuel line? What am I doing here? What are *we* doing here?"

The harshly stated questions made Drew's stomach roil. She was ready to explain, there was no good reason not to, but Orion's attitude was tough to swallow. "I wish you wouldn't be so angry."

"Angry! Lady, if you were a man right now, I'd lay you out!" Nick fumbled with the door and finally got the latch unlocked. Pushing the door open, he jumped to the ground.

Drew sat where she was, stiffly, numbly. She had no immediate solution to the situation, and Orion was trekking around the brushy clearing with the jerky movements of an enraged grizzly. Fat lot of good *that* would do!

Watching Orion storm around, Drew irrationally took note of the man's excellent physique, his broad shoulders, his lean hips, his long legs. He was wearing jeans, black cowboy boots, a white shirt and a tan suede vest. He must be well over six feet tall, she thought, while worrying her bottom lip with her teeth.

She sat up straighter as he turned around and came back to the copter. Her door was yanked open. "Why'd you want me out here?" Instead of waiting for an explanation, Nick's narrowed gaze swept the area. "Just how in hell are we going to get out of here?'' His hard blue eyes landed on her again. ''Got any suggestions, baby?''

With that one sarcastically drawled word, *baby,* he'd aligned her with every female airhead who'd ever been born. Drew had grown up with a pair of overbearing older brothers, and female censure wasn't at all unfamiliar to her. But she'd learned to fight back, too, and this man standing there and digging at her very foundation, when he had no idea what kind of woman she really was, was too much.

Maybe she had caused their present predicament, but she hadn't done it intentionally, and she wasn't an airhead and she wasn't a ''baby,'' not in the insulting sense Orion had just labeled her.

''Let me out,'' she demanded, wriggling from the seat and maneuvering one boot into the recessed foothold. Orion stood by and watched her descend without offering assistance, which suited Drew just fine. She wouldn't have accepted his hand if he'd begged to help her down!

Standing on the ground, however, was a decided disadvantage, she realized when she had to tilt back her head to glare at Orion's face. That was okay, too. She wasn't afraid of the man just because he was twice her size. Judd and Simon were both big bruisers, and she'd never backed down from a confrontation with either of them.

Of course, they did as they pleased, like trying to sell the ranch without her approval. It's two against one, they'd told her, a majority vote, and none of her arguments were swaying their determination.

''Look,'' she said with a well-defined scowl. ''I'm sorry. I never intended putting you in any kind of jeopardy. But I don't have to listen to slurs on my intelligence!''

Nick's hands were on his hips in a deprecating pose. "I'm supposed to believe your great intelligence got us into this mess? Come off it, lady! Or hasn't it sunk in, yet, that we're stranded out here? Maybe that's it. Maybe you haven't figured out that there's no phone, no radio, and with your damned shenanigans, I'll bet no one even knows where we are!''

He was a fighter, too, Drew realized. His anger wasn't phony. He was mad through and through. She drew a deep breath. "So yelling at me is going to help? Insulting me is going to help?''

Nick walked away, both hands raking his hair. His gaze took in their utter isolation, the miles and miles of trees and mountains and brush and...the house! He turned back to Drew. "Your brothers still use the place for hunting, don't they?''

She nodded sullenly. Orion's smugly superior attitude had succeeded in raising her hackles to the point of intense dislike.

"Then there could be some supplies."

"There are. They always leave canned goods and staples up here. You won't starve, Mr. Orion," she drawled.

"You might think that's funny, Miss Smartass, but what if no one figures out where we are for a couple of days?''

"Days?'' Drew swallowed hard. Her own fears hadn't gone quite that far yet. Days out here with this loathsome individual? What had she ever done to deserve *that* gruesome fate?

He was right about one thing, though. They wouldn't

starve, and they'd have a roof over their heads. Eventually someone would come along.

But it only made sense that any search-and-rescue operation would concentrate on the planned route for the day's flight. And that did not include the Black Creek area. Exactly what had Will Torgeson told Orion's people about the pilot switch? Torgeson's minor emergency had taken him out of the area, and did Orion's team know precisely who was piloting the helicopter today? She'd told no one—not a deliberate omission—but that's how it had worked out.

Drew's fighting spirit flagged. If she could only fix the rotor blades. The clog in the fuel line should be a simple matter, but the rotors were a whole other ball game.

At least she could inspect them and figure out just how much damage had been done, for all the good that would do. She moved back to the copter and began to climb.

"What are you doing now?"

He had the most annoying way of speaking Drew had ever heard. His questions were demands, pure and simple, irritating as all get out. "Checking the damage," she said over her shoulder, her voice dripping icicles.

There were handholds, and she'd climbed up to the engine cowling and rotor head on dozens of copters. Only on the very top of the machine could one make a close inspection of the blades.

But she felt herself slipping down the fuselage, one foot losing traction and then the other. "Yipes!" she cried as she lost hold completely and started dropping.

Big hands closed around her bottom, clamping her

to the side of the copter. "Stop it!" she yelled. "Let me down!"

"Let you fall? What are you, some kind of nut?"

And then she heard a sort of half growl, half chuckle behind her. Orion was getting some kind of perverted kick out of hanging on to her behind! Drew felt blood rushing to her face. She couldn't be in a more humiliating situation if she'd tried!

"If you'd let go of me, I could slide the rest of the way to the ground," she said through clenched teeth.

"How long have you been a pilot?" The question was put sarcastically, implying very distinctly that anyone as inept as she was couldn't possibly be an old hand with a copter.

Drew nearly choked on a sudden rush of fury. But she wasn't going to start reciting her training and experience to this insufferable man at this debasing moment. "I hardly think we're in any position to make small talk!"

"My position's not so bad."

"Well, mine stinks! Dammit, Orion, let go of my... Let go of *me!*"

Nick almost laughed. If the whole situation weren't so damned irritating, he might have cut loose with a good laugh. It served this conniving female right to be clinging to the side of the copter three feet off the ground.

Besides, she felt pretty good. She wasn't very big— not tall, at least—and her figure was blatantly female, her hips, especially. Nick liked a woman with a little meat on her bones, and Drew LeBeau's softly padded posterior was just about perfect in his estimation.

She had on tan slacks, laced brown ankle-high boots and an overlarge cream-colored sweatshirt. It was plain, quite ordinary clothing that looked more than ordinary, somehow.

No matter, Drew LeBeau was a pain in the neck, a *dangerous* pain in the neck. As first impressions went, she had made one he'd never forget.

Drew thought of giving him a good kick, then thought again. They were alone out here, and kicking someone, an already angry man, especially, probably wouldn't be the smartest thing a woman could do.

"All right, enough's enough," she fumed. "Take your hands off me this second!"

Nick hesitated, then decided to do exactly as she demanded. Releasing her abruptly, he stepped back for the fall. Sure enough, she hit the ground, landing on her seat. He saw the impact in her eyes, but she never so much as flinched. Chalk one up for her, he thought grudgingly, admitting that whatever else she was, she was pretty darned gutsy.

Drew scrambled to her feet and dusted off her slacks. She was embarrassed but would die on the spot before letting Orion know. "I'm going to the house," she stated defiantly, as though anticipating some more of Orion's scathing disapproval.

"Fine. Do whatever you want. I have a feeling that's your style, babe, just barreling into trouble full speed ahead."

"That's *not*..." Drew stopped the angry flow of words, turned and marched away. Orion had a point, and she knew it, but it was always the truth that hurt. Not that she normally looked for trouble, but after today's fiasco there was little chance of proving it to Nick Orion.

"Trouble with a capital *T*," Nick muttered to himself, watching her go. She was mad as hell.

Well, so was he. They were in a fine fix, and just how long would it take George and the rest of the crew to figure out he might be here and come looking?

TWO

The house wasn't locked, which was normal procedure. Drew pushed the front door open and wrinkled her nose at the musty odor of the place. Each visit for Drew included an airing out, and she began to open windows. No one used the house very much anymore. Judd and Simon and their buddies came up during hunting season, and once in a while the LeBeau brothers brought their wives and kids up for an overnighter or a picnic in good weather.

The first ten years of Drew's life had been spent on the ranch. But then beef prices had drastically fluctuated for a period and her parents had sold the cattle and moved to Laramie. Drew knew, too, that she'd been an influencing factor in their decision. It hadn't mattered with the boys, the elder LeBeaus had felt, but a girl should have the advantages of town living.

Oddly enough, it wasn't the boys who'd always had

the strongest affinity for the Black Creek area. Drew felt something here that was missing from any other place she'd ever been. It was impossible for her to live so far out, but she drove to the ranch whenever she could find the time, sometimes bringing a friend along, sometimes making the trip by herself.

The best pieces of furniture had been moved to Laramie long ago, and what had been left behind hadn't been cared for with any degree of concern. Chairs and tables were mismatched and scarred, the carpet was worn and stained in spots, and the walls and woodwork were faded and tinged with age. It was just another deserted ranch, far, far into the mountains, isolated, neglected and all but forgotten.

That's why Judd and Simon had decided to sell, or at least the reason they'd given Drew. She'd come unglued the first time they'd mentioned it, which hadn't altered her brothers' staunch attitude. After several noisy but futile arguments, she'd begged them to at least sell to someone who would keep the ranch intact.

But that plea hadn't gone anywhere, either. "Orion's offered a good price and no one else wants the place, Drew. No one. Can't you understand that?"

Drew didn't believe it. Her brothers hadn't put the ranch on the open market; Orion had come to them. But with some advertisement, who knew who might come along and fall in love with the place? If she had the money, she would buy her brothers' shares and keep the ranch for the rest of her life.

But she didn't begin to have that kind of money.

Drew walked through the sparsely furnished living room to the kitchen. A quick inspection of the cabinets' contents evidenced more than enough food for two people for several days. Orion wouldn't be dining elegantly, by any stretch of the imagination, but he wouldn't go hungry.

And there would be electricity and running water if she could get the ancient motor in the well house started. It was an eccentric old thing, sometimes coughing to life on the first try and sometimes remaining frustratingly silent through a dozen attempts.

That would be her first chore, Drew decided, going through the back door and down the path to the well house. Orion was a nasty, unlikable person, but he wouldn't be in this unholy situation without her pushy intrusion into his life. She was sorry for what she'd done, although no one could have foreseen a near accident merely because she had added a slight detour to Orion's schedule. Neither of them was in the slightest danger now, but they had been, and if Orion had been injured…?

A shudder shook Drew's body. Visualizing what could have happened was horrifying enough to give her the shakes for weeks to come. She would think long and hard before allowing emotion to influence her judgment in the future.

Putting regret aside for the time being, however, Orion was her responsibility. As aggravating as he was, she would dutifully see to his comfort during their forced stay out here. It wasn't a matter of making amends; his forgiveness was highly unlikely, whatever lengths she went to.

But she took responsibility seriously, whatever Orion might think of her. He would have hot water and food, and should they still be here at nightfall—a repugnant but more than probable likelihood—he would have a decent bed.

Symbolically rolling up her sleeves, Drew entered the dank little well house to tackle the old motor.

Nick was walking around the lifeless helicopter, making note of the new scratches it bore and worrying about rescue and how long he'd be stuck out here. Drew LeBeau was a threat to civilized society. He could raise merry hell with her pilot's license, he knew. The FAA didn't take this sort of stunt lightly, and if anyone deserved to be grounded it was a bubbleheaded female who thought nothing of virtually kidnapping a man and then nearly killing him in a dangerous landing in a pile of brush.

Well, maybe "kidnapping" was a bit strong. She had asked if he minded the detour, and then asked again if he would object to landing at the ranch. Everything seemed to have happened so fast after that—the sputtering engine, Drew's decision that putting down was no longer a matter of choice.

What seemed to be lodged in Nick's brain was a suspicion that Drew had engineered the whole thing.

He didn't want to know her reason, Nick told himself, muttering under his breath. He didn't want to hear any excuses, explanations or pleas. And he just might contact the FAA and file that complaint when he got back to Laramie, damned woman!

Nick's angry gaze rose to the vacant blue sky. George, being the efficient guy he was, had probably already discovered that the company helicopter was missing. He was no doubt checking the various development sites to look for him. Once George concluded that the copter had to have gone down somewhere, he would contact the authorities and begin a search. Had

Drew LeBeau considered how much worry she had caused today? Her own brothers would be panicked!

To Nick, the worst aspect of his conjecture was that Black Creek Ranch hadn't been a part of the day's planned agenda. It could be a while before anyone thought to check this range of mountains.

Unless Drew had told someone—anyone—what she was doing today. Nick tried to recall their limited conversation. He'd mentioned no one knowing where they were and she hadn't rebutted the charge. But there was still the chance she might have said something to someone.

It was too crucial to overlook, Nick decided, turning abruptly and heading for the house.

He'd been inside the house only one time before, during one of his visits to inspect the property. The old structure wasn't important to his development plans, although he had been considering using it for an on-the-site sales office.

It was a creaky old place, with dull wood siding and a shake roof. Very outdated. Even for temporary office usage, it would need extensive repairs.

Nick walked in. The front door opened on the living room, and he stopped for a second to admire the native rock fireplace, which took up one entire wall. The house had few redeeming features, but that fireplace was something special. He'd forgotten it until seeing it again.

Everything was quiet. "Drew?" he yelled. Even saying her name riled him. What he should be calling her was Trouble. Hey, Trouble, he should shout. Come on, Trouble, where are you?

And it made him grin grimly to realize that he was presently looking for "Trouble."

His spurt of amusement quickly disappeared as he went to the kitchen. There was nothing funny about today's events. He'd had a dozen tasks planned, every one of them important and necessary to his operation. His success in a tough field wasn't an accident, a co-incidence or a piece of luck. He'd worked his butt off the past four years, seven days a week, fifty-two weeks a year.

And he resented Drew LeBeau for interrupting his tight schedule more than he could ever remember resenting anything.

The back door had been left ajar. Nick walked out onto the porch and stopped. The view from this spot was mind-boggling, which was the other redeeming feature of the old house, he remembered now. During his previous visit, he'd stood right here for several minutes, just drinking in the incredible scenery.

But he'd also added up profits. People loved to own a piece of this kind of land—city people, especially. They came from Los Angeles and Detroit and Chicago, drawn by his ads in sports and outdoor magazines, and they fell in love with Wyoming. To own a piece of it was a dream come true, and they took home photos and memories of their very own twenty or forty acres.

A clanking sound, and then the rattling of a motor starting up, drew Nick's attention away from the view. The racket came from a small building at the end of a path, and Nick headed down the porch steps and walked toward it. Before he reached the open door of the shed, the motor settled down to a steadier rumble. He peered in to see Drew bending over a sizable con-traption with an assortment of moving belts and gears.

For a moment the small, shapely woman stood out in the dusky surroundings. Her crop of shiny hair and rounded derriere particularly appealed to his masculinity. Her slacks weren't a bit too tight, but standing as she was, the tan fabric was as smooth as a second skin, distinctly defining what could only be described as a great behind.

It was the second time he'd noticed that, and it seemed to Nick like an extraordinary lack of good sense on his part. Forgetting Drew LeBeau's exasperating disposition for even a minute would be a mistake. Thinking men stayed away from troublesome women, and he'd already decided—adamantly—that this woman epitomized trouble.

He forced his gaze to the growling motor. It was the old diesel-fueled engine that generated electricity for the house and powered the water pump, of course, which Drew had obviously been busily starting. Nick could see grease on her hands and a smudge on her face. She could have asked for help, but had she? Oh, no, not this female!

Her independence was grating. Everything about her was grating. The last hour rushed Nick again, every wretched second of it. "Looking for something else to wreak your particular brand of havoc on?" he drawled.

Drew spun around. "You shouldn't sneak up on a person like that!" And then his belittling question sank in. "Do you want indoor plumbing? Or maybe you'd rather use the woods!"

"It's immaterial what I *use*, and none of your business!"

If it wouldn't have inconvenienced her, Drew would have killed the engine on the spot. Fat chance of this jerk getting it started again!

Gritting her teeth, she turned back to the engine and adjusted the throttle, bringing it down to a low hum of energy. Ignoring Orion's threatening figure in the doorway, she flipped the switch that would start the water pump working. In a matter of minutes, the pipes in the house would fill. The hot-water tank would fill, also, and with the electricity generated from this engine, there would be hot water for showers this evening.

Orion wasn't going to thank her, but maybe she'd already known that. He probably thanked no one for anything. There were people like that, she knew, although thus far in her thirty-one years she'd met very few such cold fish.

One thing was certain: even without a crash landing, she wouldn't have gotten very far pleading to this man's sensitivity. He had none!

Drew picked up a rag and used it to wipe the grease off her hands. "Did you sneak up on me for a specific reason, or is 'sneaking' your normal approach?"

Nick ignored her sarcasm and got right to the point. "Did you tell anyone—*anyone*—you were coming here today?"

Drew continued to wipe her hands, although the question weakened her knees. If only she *had* told someone. "Afraid not."

"No one? Are you absolutely certain?"

"Positive." Drew tossed the rag. "Sorry."

Her nonchalance, as though the subject was completely inconsequential, stood Nick's hair on end. "Has it occurred to you what kind of disturbance you've caused today? Put you and me aside for the moment. We're on the ground, luckily in one piece. But no one else knows that. Copter crashes can be damned serious. People will be scouring the Laramie area, taking chances to look for us. Your harebrained antics could get someone else hurt, and if nothing else, today is going to waste a lot of people's time and money.''

Drew was getting more uncomfortable by the second. She'd thought of what would happen in Laramie once someone realized the copter wasn't where it should be. She'd taken part in several search-and-rescue operations herself, and knew how much energy and dedication people expended on such endeavours.

Actually, if Orion weren't such a hard-nosed know-it-all, she might have collapsed from worry long before this, although that really wasn't her style. She was trying to be practical, and his relentless needling seemed to be working opposite to what he undoubtedly hoped for. He'd like to see her weeping, Drew realized, groveling, begging his forgiveness. Was that what he liked in a woman, helplessness, a simpering I'm-so-sorry-I-could-die attitude?

Well, she *was* sorry, but she wasn't helpless and she'd never simpered in her life. An emotional decline might satisfy Orion's thirst for revenge, but the only thing it would do for her was make her nauseous.

''I know what's going on in Laramie better than you do,'' she told him coldly. ''How many search-and-rescue operations have *you* volunteered time for?''

Nick took a quick step backward as she swept out of the well house with an imperious thrust of her chin. She was the feistiest little woman he'd ever met, as irritating as a swarm of gnats, as vexing as an unsolvable puzzle.

He didn't follow her into the house. If she made one more smart-ass crack, he was apt to forget her gender, and it was infuriating, in itself, that she had the power to make him even think of such a thing.

* * *

Drew marched through the house, using it as the most direct route to reach the copter again. Climbing up into the cabin, she gathered up her flight bag and lightweight jacket and jumped back down to the ground. She never flew without a few essentials, a longtime habit that had proven beneficial on more than one occasion.

This was one of them, obviously. The flight bag contained a set of fresh underwear, some cosmetics, a small tube of hand lotion and a toothbrush, just common, everyday items that would unquestionably lessen the stress she was in for until rescue.

If Orion had nothing at all with him—his briefcase was still in the rear seat and who knew what it contained?—that was his problem. In fact, it would do his stiff-necked personality good for him to go unshaven for a few days.

Drew paused to scan the empty sky, her stomach lurching uncomfortably. Wouldn't someone in Orion's organization come up with the possibility of Orion having decided to drop in on Black Creek during his scheduled tour?

It might take a little time for everyone to get together, for Judd and Simon to realize that not only was Orion's copter missing, but so was their sister. A little investigation and communication would place her as Orion's pilot for the day.

Drew made a worried face: she should have made sure that Torgeson planned to relate the name of the pilot taking his place today. It would be much easier to add two and two if everyone knew that Drew LeBeau was at the controls.

She'd gotten so excited when Will had asked her to handle Orion's flight. Not once had it occurred to her that something like this might happen. She racked up thousands of miles in the air for the Forest Service every year, a job she loved. Would that be in jeopardy, too, because of today's foolishness?

Listlessly, Drew started back to the house with her possessions. She'd made her bed and she had to lie in it. Orion's anger was irritatingly justified and she'd do her best to tolerate it. He wouldn't be stuck out here without her interference. Fighting back was a lifelong habit, however. Judd and Simon had conditioned her to defend herself from the time she could walk and talk, and there were distinct similarities between their over-bearing machismo and Orion's.

Not that she didn't love her big, gruff brothers. But she knew where she stood with them. Females were the weaker sex, males were dominant, rarely wrong and always, *always,* in control. The women they'd married seemed to enjoy their husband's distorted sense of fair play. Drew did not. She'd battled her brothers' chau-vinistic tendencies all her life.

Nick Orion was the same kind of man, she felt, overly confident, too damned good-looking, and posi-tive of his superiority over the opposite sex. Her time in his presence was going to be a gut-wrenching ex-perience, one that she'd undoubtedly remember for the rest of her life.

But she'd caused it herself, and she'd live through it. Somehow.

Inside the house again, Drew went to the bedroom area. Of the four bedrooms, there was one she always used during her visits, and she dropped her jacket and flight bag on the familiar blue spread. This bed was made up, but it was the only one with sheets, blankets and pillows already in place.

A hall closet contained plenty of bedding, and she took out a set and brought it to the bedroom farthest away from hers. There was only one bathroom, and Orion would have to share it with her, like it or not.

After making up Orion's bed, Drew found an old towel and dusted the top of the dresser in his room. She gave a quick swipe to the plain wood chair and the small nightstand beside the bed, then went down the hall to the bathroom to inspect its condition.

She had water, she noted gratefully with a turn of a faucet. It took about ten minutes to wipe down the bathroom fixtures, then she laid out some clean blue towels on the left side of the sink and some red ones on the right.

A glance in the mirror was anything but rewarding. She looked frazzled, no matter how hard she'd been trying to remain cool. She ran her fingers through her short hair, noting that the lipstick she'd used that morning was totally gone. Her green eyes had a pale cast and her mouth seemed tight and pinched.

Ordinarily, Drew didn't worry too much about her looks, but staring at her reflection, she found herself wondering how Orion saw her. Then, instantly annoyed at such silly speculation, she stuck her tongue out at the mirror. Who cared what Orion thought? His type of man usually liked women leggy and brainless, two things she could never be!

Now came the hard part, Drew thought with a heavy sigh as she left the bathroom and headed for the kitchen. She had taken care of the few chores needed to make the house usable. From here on in, it was a matter of waiting for someone to come along. There would be meals to fix, of course, but it didn't require much time, intelligence or energy to wield a can opener.

At the kitchen window she saw Orion walking around outside. Pacing. The man moved as if he was driven to be doing something, as though he'd curl up and die if he sat down and just relaxed. Didn't he know how to relax?

Relaxation was the beauty of this place. Didn't he feel it? The serenity of the dark green forest and distant mountain peaks? She was under stress, too, but she could still appreciate the utter quiet, the fresh pine smell drifting on the gentle breezes, the peace.

Maybe she should show him that sitting back with one's feet up wouldn't cause the world to come to an abrupt end.

Then, again, this probably wasn't the most auspicious time to be taunting Nick Orion. Although if ever a man needed tormenting, it was him.

Well, she wouldn't deliberately rile him, but she had every right to sit on the back porch and look at the view.

Drew slipped quietly out the back door and sat down. There were three old chairs on the porch, situated expressly for doing nothing. They were there for relaxation, for looking at the panorama of mountains and sky. For cloud watching.

She saw Orion look her way and quickly, stubbornly turn his back. He's impossible, she thought, with a cynical shake of her head, and tipped her chair onto its back legs so she could rest her feet on the porch railing.

Her eyes scanned the horizon. Over that big, dark ridge to her left was another ranch. Using the less than strategically placed gravel and dirt roads in the area, that ranch was an awfully long way away. As the crow

flies, however, a good, experienced hiker could probably reach it in a day.

Walking out of there wasn't an impossible feat.
Drew had never attempted it, nor had her brothers, that
she knew of. But as a last resort, if too much time
passed and no one figured out where they were, she
could do it, she felt.

Orion couldn't. Only someone familiar with the
rough, rugged terrain wouldn't get lost. From this van-
tage point, directions were as distinct as Drew's own
hand, but down among the thick growth of trees and
brush, everything looked much different.

It made better sense to wait, Drew knew. At least
for a while.

Oh, oh, she thought as Orion bore down on the
porch. "How far away is the nearest neighbor?" he
questioned in a flat, unfriendly tone of voice.

Drew dropped the chair's front legs to the floor.
"I've never checked the mileage."

"Within walking distance?"

Drew shrugged. "Anything's within walking distance. Depends on your point of view."

Nick struggled with impatience. "Two miles? Ten?
A hundred?"

"You know it's not a hundred! But if you're thinking of walking out of here, forget it."

"I'm not going to stand around and do nothing!"

Drew eyed his handsome cowboy boots. "Those
weren't exactly designed for hiking," she wryly
pointed out.

It was the God's truth, and something that had been
worrying Nick. His boots were comfortable for normal
usage, but they weren't hiking boots, not by a long

shot. If he made it two miles without blisters, it would be a miracle.

But that's why he was trying to yank information on distances out of Drew LeBeau. Nick reached into his vest pocket for his roll of antacid tablets and popped two of them into his mouth. He tried again with Drew, controlling his temper only by intense concentration. "If it wouldn't be too much trouble, would you please tell me how far away your nearest neighbor is located?"

Why, he sounded almost human! And he had even said please. Imagine that.

Drew wasn't about to tell him that by cutting through the mountains, one could probably reach the Hoskins ranch in a day. He'd probably take off walking right this minute and end up hopelessly lost. There weren't that many hours left until nightfall, anyway, and him wandering around in the dark in those woods was horrifying, even to her.

Whether he believed it or not, she was going to see that Nick Orion got back to Laramie in the same heartless but physically sound condition he was in right now. And only she needed to know that if all else failed, she would set out very early one morning and hike to the Hoskins place.

"There are no neighbors. You drove up here a couple of times, didn't you? Did you see any houses?"

He hadn't, none that he could remember. But, then, he hadn't been looking for any, either. The roads wandered through these mountains in a confusing pattern. Judd had given him a detailed hand-drawn map, but he couldn't recall much of it.

Nick rubbed his mouth thoughtfully. He'd wracked his brain for a way out of this mess yet today, and

Drew LeBeau was sitting there looking as calm as could be. It didn't seem to bother her an iota that they were stranded, which was intensely irritating. Maybe she really had messed around with the fuel supply, just so she could land the bird!

He walked away, just turned his back and strode away. He felt so frustrated, so crippled. To be forced to do nothing about a problem, was the most incredibly defeating sensation he'd ever experienced.

Drew frowned at the telling lines of Orion's slumped shoulders. The man was totally crushed, and her normal compassion suddenly kicked in. She got to her feet. "Mr. Orion! Nick!" He stopped and looked back at her. "I could make a pot of coffee. Would you like a cup?"

"Is there any tea?" He'd love a cup of coffee, but the burning in his stomach precluded any such notion.

She nodded. "There might be. Let me check." Drew swung into the house and started opening cabinets. She found a tin of tea in the second one and then yelled out the door, "There's tea. It'll be ready in a couple of minutes."

Three

When the tea was hot and brown and tempting Drew's own palate, she went to the screen door to let Orion know. He'd stopped pacing, but instead of sitting down somewhere, he was leaning his tense frame against the trunk of a tall pine tree near the well house.

Drew took the opportunity to study the man. He was both handsome and much too stern-looking. Granted, there was little reason for levity at the present, but did he even know how to smile? Was his life so restricted to work—that's what she'd heard—that he enjoyed nothing else?

Absently toying with the hair above her left ear, Drew pondered a strange idea: how many days would it take for the peace of this place to affect Nick Orion? How long would he have to be isolated from his usual routines to relax? To smile, not for any particular reason, but just because he felt like smiling?

"The tea's ready," she called. "Would you like it on the porch or inside?"

Nick pushed away from the tree and walked toward the house. "The porch is fine."

Hooking a finger through the handles of two mugs and picking up the pot of tea with her other hand, Drew shouldered the screen door open and stepped out on the porch.

While Orion came up the stairs and then stood by, Drew filled the mugs. She held one out. "Here you are."

Nick took the mug, uncomfortably aware of his proximity to Drew. "Thanks." LeBeau's green eyes were deep, impenetrable, saying nothing and yet somehow communi-cating in that mysterious way women had. And there were those little laugh lines at her eyes' outer corners—almost an extension of her long, dark lashes—that he'd noticed before.

She was a pretty woman, he reluctantly admitted again, with smooth skin and a well-defined mouth. She had a small, slightly upturned nose, wide-set eyes, and her honey blond hair swept back from her short forehead in a casual, carefree style.

Something stirred within him, a typically masculine response to an attractive woman, and Nick shifted his weight, denying the sensation. If he ever decided to alter his stringent regimen of work before women, it wasn't going to happen because of Drew LeBeau.

Sipping the hot tea with some caution, he moved away from Drew. With his back to her, he stood at the railing and looked at the view.

"Sit down," Drew invited, seating herself. Civility only made sense, she felt. If Orion unbent, so would she.

"I'm fine right here."

He'd spoken without turning. He wasn't completely blocking the wide view, of course, but showing her his back was annoying, subtly insulting. Drew told herself to ignore it and sipped from her mug. Obviously Orion hadn't declared a truce just because he'd accepted a cup of tea. He was frustrated, completely unresigned. If he came up with an even slightly feasible way to get out of here, he'd try it in a heartbeat.

At least he wasn't criticizing or denouncing her now, which could merely be a temporary respite. Cross him at all, Drew suspected, and his anger would unfurl again.

Still, an uneasy silence was tough for her to maintain. Not that she was an overly chatty person. But when two people were miles away from anyone else, *some* communication was necessary.

"I made up a bed for you," she finally volunteered, supposing that news might be welcome.

Nick stiffened. "Don't go to any trouble."

"Making a bed is very little trouble."

He smirked at the scenery. This was not an ordinary situation, and LeBeau's attempt to make it seem so galled him. It infuriated him that he would have to put up with her until he got out of here. Any sharing of meals or space was going to be a test of his temper, and once this miserable ordeal was over, he never wanted to set eyes on Drew LeBeau again.

Drew was becoming a little more agitated by the minute. It seemed only sensible to regard the situation pragmatically. Neither of them wanted to be here—or rather, Orion didn't. From her point of view, sitting on this porch amid the most beautiful scenery in the western hemisphere was hardly a hardship. Orion standing there as if he had a stick up his spine and radiating bitterness was ridiculous. Hadn't he ever had to roll with the punches before? Was he completely inflexible?

Nick Orion was to be pitied, Drew thought with a small frown, although he'd probably explode if she even hinted at such a thing. But the man was the most miserably unhappy individual she'd ever been around. He had no sense of humor whatsoever and no adaptability. Just look at the way he was standing, as rigid as a board.

"You know," she said with a note of humor, unable to keep quiet another second. "You might as well sit down and relax. Glaring at those mountains isn't going to do anything but give you worry wrinkles."

Nick thought of heading down the road, tight boots and all. Blisters just might be a welcome exchange for Drew LeBeau's brand of wit. Worry wrinkles. Good Lord.

Another silent stretch ensued, and Drew was beginning to get mad. "Stop ignoring me!" she demanded. "I'm here, whether you like it or not."

Nick turned around with a cold expression. "I know you're here, believe me. But you and I don't have one damned thing to say to each other." Drew had left the teapot on a chair, and he picked it up and refilled his mug. Then, with the mug in his hand, he walked off the porch and disappeared around the side of the house.

Drew sat there dumbfounded. Apparently Orion was going to make her pay through the nose for having him in this vicinity when the copter's fuel line acted up. Normal conversation was out. He would drink her tea and probably eat whatever she put on the table. But leniency wasn't in his makeup. He despised her and didn't even try to hide it.

She inhaled slowly, a long breath that had a little-girl-hurt quality to it. How could anyone be so hard? So censuring?

Her narrowed, disgruntled gaze fell on the distant ridge that ultimately led to the Hoskins ranch. Walk out of here for Nick Orion? Never! If it took weeks for Judd and Simon or anyone else to figure out where Orion and she were, she wouldn't lift one finger to hurry the process.

The day Nick Orion relented and treated her like a human being, she might reconsider, Drew decided. Until then, he could pace and prowl and be as nasty as he chose. She didn't mind being here one little bit, and if he'd loosen up, he just might discover that there was a lot more to life than working oneself into a stupor!

Darkness was falling. Drew stood at the kitchen sink and absorbed the spectacular orange-and-pink sunset. She'd seen nothing of Orion for hours and pride wouldn't allow her to go looking for him. If he'd taken off walking, he'd realize the stupidity of that idea all on his own.

What were Judd and Simon doing this evening? Drew was deeply troubled about the worry she had caused her family. Lord help her, it hadn't been done intentionally. All she'd wanted was an hour of Orion's time, and even with the other stops on his schedule, they would have been back in Laramie before dinner.

The old house never had had a telephone. Drew remembered her parents wanting one, but the telephone lines didn't run way out here and it would have cost the LeBeau family a small fortune to install a system.

Money had never been overly abundant for the Le-
Beaus, which was probably the main reason Judd and
Simon were so eager to sell the ranch.

Drew sighed and turned away from the window.
Money was the cause of so many problems. Those that
didn't have it wanted it, and those that did wanted
more.

Her parents hadn't been like that, though. Neither
had Judd and Simon until recently. Not until Nick
Orion had come around offering an impressive sum for
the LeBeau ranch.

She'd thought about it, of course. Her salary was
pretty generous, but her third of the sale price would
provide a new car and any number of luxuries she did
without now.

A new car could never replace the ranch, she had
quickly decided, which had, of course, been the beginning of today's fiasco.

Drew opened a cabinet and surveyed her choices for
dinner. Her stomach was growling, and wherever Orion
was, he had to be hungry, too.

Judd was a chili nut. He bought his favorite brand
by the case, which accounted for the dozen or so cans
of chili in the cabinet. Drew took out two and set them
on the counter. She found the can opener and the tin
of crackers and placed those items beside the chili.

Then she hesitated. Should she give Orion a little
longer before heating up dinner?

Drew puttered while worrying the matter, absent-
mindedly organizing the canned chili, soups, vegeta-
bles and fruits in the cabinet. From a "polite society"
point of view, Orion deserved no courtesy, whatsoever.
Not that this was a drawing-room situation. But why
make matters worse by behaving like a sullen child?

Drew suspected he was staying away from the house just to avoid her, which seemed too adolescent for words. What if they were here for several days or, God forbid, a week?

The sound of the front door opening and closing announced Orion's return. Drew shut the cabinet door very quietly and tiptoed across the room. A magazine was already open on the table, and she sat down and put on an absorbed expression.

Orion's boot steps came closer, then halted at the kitchen doorway. Drew lifted her eyes to the man. He looked tired, drained. There was dust on his boots and on the hems of his jeans. What on earth had he been doing all afternoon? She saw his gaze flick to the cans of chili on the counter and back to her.

Drew cleared her throat. "I was about to make dinner." She smiled faintly and gestured to the counter. "Such as it is."

"I'm not hungry. Which bedroom is mine?"

A fist clenched in Drew's middle. Not hungry? Of course he was hungry. Unless he'd been eating grass and twigs, his stomach had to be as empty as hers!

He was carrying his briefcase, looking as distant and cold as a January moon. "Which bedroom?"

Astonishment made her stammer. "Uh...the one at the end of the hall."

"Thanks."

Drew got unsteadily to her feet as Orion vanished from the doorway. She could hear him in the hall, and then the slam of the bedroom door. Her emotions were flipping around, an incredible array of them. Orion's unyielding, unforgiving attitude was unique to her experiences with either sex. Anger was a natural reaction to a frustrating situation, but guarding that anger, clinging to it the way Orion seemed to be doing, was astounding.

Shaking her head in disgust, Drew went to the counter and picked up the can opener. Orion might be pouting to the point of going to bed without supper, but she was hungry!

Drew turned over in bed and listened. Thunder was rumbling through the heavens and rain was pattering on the roof—a summer storm had awakened her. She snuggled deeper into the blankets, luxuriating in the comfort and warmth of the old bed.

The room lit up with a flash of lightning. The storm was welcome. She loved rain on the roof at night, and the area needed a good soaking.

Was Orion awake and listening, too?

Drew sighed. The man was an enigma, an impossible irritant one minute and arousing compassion the next. He had come out of the bedroom one time before she had retired for the night, to take a shower. With the house so quiet, there was no mistaking the sound of the shower running. Then he'd again vanished behind the solidly closed door of his assigned bedroom and Drew had sat at the kitchen table and thumbed through old magazines until she'd gotten sleepy.

Face it, she told herself in the darkness now. You don't know how to deal with a man like Orion. Judd and Simon are gold-haloed angels compared to him, and you've always thought them to be the most dedicated pair of male chauvinists in North America. Next to Nick Orion, Judd and Simon are rookies, amateurs.

Oddly, Drew's thoughts became personally slanted. Orion had a lot to offer in the way of physical appeal. She functioned normally, and rarely failed to notice an outstandingly good-looking man. Granted, Orion's looks were flawed by his ridiculously implacable personality. But it was hard not to appreciate electric blue eyes, thick, dark hair and a strong, athletic body, all the same.

And she couldn't doubt his intelligence. The man had brains, obviously. No one accomplished what he had in the business world without a goodly amount of gray matter.

But what did he do for fun? At the end of a long day, what sort of amusements did he look for? Regardless of gossip about his overly zealous work ethics, Orion had to have other interests. Everyone did.

She loved to dance, for example. And work jigsaw puzzles when she had the time. And read, and have friends over to the house for impromptu potluck dinners. She liked parlor games, and high-school football and basketball, and she loved driving up here for a weekend. There was always something to do outside her job, which she also enjoyed.

Her job. Drew's heart sank. Orion could cause her a lot of trouble. She had put her pilot's license on the line today. Inadvertently, granted, but facts were facts: she had deliberately strayed from a formal flight schedule. Ordinarily she wasn't so reckless. Torgeson's call had triggered her imagination, apparently, and her plan had seemed completely logical.

Drew knew she was wavering again. Getting Orion back to Laramie as fast as possible was her best course. She should get up very early and set out for the Hoskins ranch.

The storm was getting worse, she realized uneasily. The woods were getting drenched, and if it rained all night, some of the creeks would be flooded and impassable, Black Creek especially.

A discordant sound brought Drew's head up from the pillow. Orion must be up. Good Lord, did the man pace in his sleep, too?

Drew strained to listen. Orion must have gone outside, through the kitchen door. She couldn't resist, and she scrambled out of bed to furtively approach the window, which looked out on the back porch.

Orion was standing near the rail, staring off at the rain, Drew supposed. His white shirt wasn't buttoned or tucked into his jeans, as though he'd awakened and had felt a hasty need to see the storm firsthand.

It did present new problems, Drew had to agree. A heavy rainfall was confining, and should it turn into a real downpour, she wouldn't dare attempt to cross Black Creek by herself.

Things could be worse, but right at the moment it was tough for Drew to see how. She chewed on a thumbnail while she watched Orion. Battered emotions aside, he was a beautiful man. If she'd met him under other circumstances, through a friend, or even because of Judd and Simon, wouldn't she have been just a little bit starry-eyed?

Every one of Drew's romances had been brief and ultimately disappointing. She had watched her friends fall in love and get married one by one and, yes, she'd wondered if it would ever happen to her. Her brothers had told her on more than one occasion that she was too picky, which was probably true. She honestly didn't know what she expected from a man, other than basic, everyday decency.

Sensitivity? Consideration for others? Great stuff, if

you could get it. She had come to believe those qualities were rare, and not only in men.

For that matter, labeling what she'd done today as either sensitive or considerate would be a distortion of the truth. She had flung herself into Orion's life, nearly getting him killed in the process and unquestionably creating a situation without recourse. If he was angry, he should be, and if he couldn't stand the sight of her, maybe she deserved that, too.

Tears filled Drew's eyes, and she left the window and crawled back into bed. She rarely cried. Judd and Simon had thickened her skin years ago. She had learned to stand her ground, to fight rather than cry, to give back whatever people dished out. It had always worked before.

She felt like an utter fool, and she buried her face into the pillow and wept.

Drew slept fretfully the rest of the night, hearing the incessant rain even when she did sleep. She awoke finally, to a gray light instead of sunshine, and dragged herself out of bed with very little enthusiasm.

The house was quiet. Orion could be anywhere, still in bed—which she doubted—outside, or in any given room. For the first time since the near accident, Drew wished it were possible to completely avoid facing Nick Orion again.

The temperature had dropped drastically, she realized as she shivered into her clothes. Dressed, she opened her bedroom door and peered down the hall. It was empty, so she went on to the bathroom.

A few minutes later Drew headed for the kitchen. The smell of coffee drifted on the air, indicating that

Orion had not only gotten up first, he'd found the coffeepot.

It surprised her, however, to see him sitting at the kitchen table. "Good morning," popped out of her mouth before she could stop it.

"Morning."

She cast him a wary glance and got a mug out of the cabinet. Orion didn't look any different than yesterday, but something about him *felt* different. And he had answered her, almost civilly.

Drew poured her coffee into her mug. "It rained most of the night."

"It started shortly after midnight."

Apparently he'd checked the time. Drew tried a sip from her mug. "Good coffee." He'd requested tea yesterday and she wondered about his habits.

"It's all right."

"No, really, it's very good." Drew walked over to the window and looked out. The day was gray and dismal, with heavy overhanging clouds and a fine drizzle of rain. The forest was misty, obscure, impenetrable-looking. Scratch walking out of here today, she thought.

But she wasn't going to let it get her down. Orion was speaking to her, if in a stilted manner. Her peripheral vision caught his movements as he raised his mug of coffee to his lips.

"I lived out here until I was ten," she said, almost to herself. She had memories of those years, of rainy mornings like this, of mornings during winter when her dad had to plow two, three feet of fresh snow from the road to get her and the boys to the school bus. It had been a long ride in Dad's four-wheel-drive pickup to the boarding spot, and then another long ride on the bus to school. Mornings had started very early in those days. Mom had always served a hot breakfast, bustling around this kitchen, making sure that lunches were packed and everyone got what they needed.

Drew heaved a sigh for those days, and Nick watched the rise and fall of her shoulders. His judgment of Drew LeBeau hadn't relented, but anger could be sustained only so long. He'd finally fallen asleep and had slept sounder than he could remember doing for a long spell. At first light, though, he'd awakened as usual.

He was rested and restless, physically prepared for a busy day when there was nothing to do. But frustration was waning, too, right along with anger, although he wasn't eager to begin exchanging life stories with this woman.

Receiving no response to her comment, Drew turned away from the window. "I'm going to make some pancakes. Would you like some?"

"I'll have some, thanks."

Drew put her mug of coffee on the counter and began digging out the griddle and container of pancake mix. "This is the super-easy kind," she declared. "It only needs water to liquefy it. Everything else is in the mix."

Nick nodded silently, watching her. She moved gracefully, a lulling sight for a man with nothing to do. He could have made the pancakes, he knew. He was perfectly capable of "liquefying" pancake mix and heating up a griddle.

But he'd made the coffee and then sat down. And wondered what a man without anything to do did all day, assuming he was going to be here all day, of course.

Nick set his mug down. "Your brothers—Simon and Judd. Are they going to catch on that you're missing? I mean, are the three of you close enough for them to know you're not where you should be?"

"The people I work with will probably miss me first. Yesterday was a day off, but today…?" Orion had a point, Drew realized uneasily. Judd and Simon had had no reason to contact her yesterday or last night. They *still* might not know she wasn't—as Orion had put it— where she should be.

Nick leaned forward. "When they figure it out, will they think of looking for you up here?"

"I…don't know. Eventually, I suppose," she added at Orion's crestfallen expression. "I've tried to think it through," she said quickly. "When I don't show up this morning, my supervisor might try calling my house. There's no one there, so…"

Drew thought of something. "Your people will understand what happened before mine do. Torgeson…" she hesitated, worrying again that Will might not have named his replacement before he left town "…knows I'm with you."

Nick sat back, his anger flaring again. He didn't blame Will Torgeson. Whatever had happened had been Drew's doing. Will would have stuck to the itinerary; Drew had taken it upon herself to alter it to fit her own whims. She was solely responsible for his predicament.

But this morning he wasn't in a frame of mind to walk out and leave Drew sputtering, as he'd done with her yesterday and last night.

"After your supervisor gets no answer at your house, what will he do?"

Drew rubbed her back of her neck with some nervousness. "He…might check my personnel file for an emergency number, I suppose. That would be Judd's number." Drew frowned. "I *think* I put down Judd's number."

Nick held up a restraining hand. "Judd's or Simon's, it doesn't matter. What's important is that your family will be informed of your absence. Okay, now we're getting somewhere. Put yourself in your brothers' shoes. What do you think they'll do?"

Drew sucked in a long, slow breath. She'd already tried to figure that one out. Several times. "They won't connect me to you," she said. "That's got to come from your people."

"Is George Hollister aware of who you are?"

"I've never met a George Hollister."

"He works for me. George knew I was going to have a different pilot yesterday. He mentioned it before we left the office."

"I suppose Hollister could be the person Will talked to," Drew said weakly. She hated getting anyone in trouble, even "George," whom she'd never set eyes on, and she was beginning to feel that Orion was blaming everyone even remotely connected to yesterday's pilot switch.

"Look," she said with a little more forcefulness. "No one's at fault but me. I accept full responsibility…. No, I *demand* full responsibility."

"Demand?" Nick drawled. "Lady, you've *got* full responsibility, whether you want it or not. Who else would I lay it on? Will and George are only men. How in hell would they compete with a devious mind like yours?"

Drew stepped back two full strides, completely off balance from such an insulting observation. "You don't know anything about me. Are you so perfect that you can judge other people without knowing them?''

Nick's eyes narrowed. "I know you well enough."

"Oh, you do. We've exchanged very little information about ourselves, but you know me 'well enough.' You're a very self-assured man, aren't you? Well, I can't say that I know you, but maybe it's enough, too. You're an intractable grump, and why anyone would *ever* want to know you is beyond me!" Drew turned away, wondering why she felt like bawling.

"Your personal opinion doesn't affect me a whole hell of a lot," Nick retorted. "I'm trying to figure out just how long we might be out here. I don't think a little cooperation on your part is asking too much."

Drew was dealing with anger and a ridiculous urge to cry, but she managed to glance over her shoulder and give him a fairly level look. "You don't ask, you grill!"

"And you evade!"

"I most certainly do not! What is there to evade, anyway? Do you think I wanted you out here for some...some sinister reason?"

Nick got to his feet. Drew's eyes were blazing, but so were his. "I don't know why you wanted me out here. Probably to squeeze a little more money out of me for this isolated piece of *godawful* land!"

"More money!" Drew laughed cynically. "You've got rocks in your head if that's what you think." She threw up her hands. "Think what you want." After spending time with this disgusting person, her plan looked so silly she could hardly believe she'd had any faith in it. And she certainly wasn't going to try and explain it to him now.

But there was one point she *would* explain. Drew had started to stir the pancake batter, but she dropped the spoon and whirled around to face Orion again. "Bringing you out here was a mistake, which I'm the first to admit. But it was my skill that brought us down safely, and we had no choice about landing, Orion, whether you want to believe it or not!"

She took a harried breath. "One more thing. I don't have a devious mind! I'm probably a hell of a lot less devious than a man who convinces city people who've never even seen trees outside of a manicured park to buy a chunk of undeveloped land in the wilderness!"

Four

Nick's thoughts flew in several directions. All right, fine, she was a good pilot. He'd give her that, because she *had* gotten them out of a sticky situation, but she had no right to demean his career! "The people who buy my land know exactly what they're getting," he snarled. "They buy because wilderness is what they want!"

It was a subject with personal ramifications for Drew, although she'd never once thought about greenhorns in the wilderness until Orion had come slithering into her life. Her eyes took on added fire while she pondered that one. She wasn't the only person here who'd done some "barging." Who had invited Nick Orion into *her* affairs, which was precisely what he'd done with his damned purchase offer!

To multiply his sins, she hadn't even been directly contacted! The entire deal was being negotiated with her brothers, as though her one-third ownership didn't rate recognition. Her signature would ultimately be needed, of course, but with her brothers' mulish determination, she knew darned well she'd probably sign in the end.

But Orion should have discussed the ranch with her, as well as with Judd and Simon. She had some very good ammunition for all-out war, Drew realized. She could lay it on this insufferable man and watch him squirm through the tirade. He'd fight back, and they could stand here and trade insults until they ran out of breath. Her natural spirit urged her to do it, too, to let Nick Orion have it with both barrels.

But there was something else in her system along with all that righteous indignation, an uncommon awareness of Orion's physical appeal. His good looks shouldn't matter to her, but they did.

Confused, Drew turned back to the pancake batter. Backing down from a fight was foreign to her nature and would tickle her brothers if they had witnessed it. She was glad no one had.

But someone *had* been a witness, and Nick stood there with a deeply furrowed brow while Drew stirred the pancake batter with a jerky, almost violent rhythm. She was steamed, and he was geared up for a battle, too.

They aroused intensely volatile emotions in each other, he realized. Drew LeBeau was a spitfire, a woman with a short fuse, but she had just backed off from a toe-to-toe confrontation. How come?

Nick finished off his coffee and went to the stove for a refill. Even with the near fight still in his system, his stomach wasn't burning this morning. Inviting it to act up by drinking coffee probably wasn't wise, but damn, he loved coffee!

"I'm sorry I didn't say thanks yesterday for getting us down safely," he said as he poured coffee into his mug.

Drew blinked at the batter in the bowl. Was Orion actually speaking to her in a civil tone? Apologizing? She sent him a quick glance, not all that sure she'd heard right. "Thanks for saying so now."

Nick resumed his seat at the table. "I probably should learn to fly myself," he said, and then added thoughtfully, "Might not be wise, though. Too many other things on my mind."

Drew sighed. They'd both made a mistake yesterday. Hers was more serious than Orion's, but it had been only a mistake, nonetheless. She never would have deviated from his intended flight schedule if there'd been the slightest doubt in her mind of his safety. She *was* a good pilot, cautious and conscientious. If his blasted copter hadn't developed a fuel-supply problem, she never would have attempted a landing with so much dangerous debris on the ground.

The griddle was hot, she noted, and she ladled out four small circles of batter onto the cooking surface. While the first sides were browning, she located the plastic container of syrup and brought it to the table.

"There isn't any butter," she said tonelessly, while taking down a couple of plates from a cabinet, which had been an unnecessary announcement. Orion knew there was no fresh food in the house as well as she did.

He didn't answer. When the cakes were done, she flipped all four of them onto one plate and set them in front of Orion. "What about you?" he asked.

"I'll have the next batch. Enjoy."

"Thanks."

They weren't exactly friendly toward each other, but the atmosphere in the kitchen wasn't nearly as frosty as it had been. Without comment, Nick got up and tended the griddle while Drew ate the next four cakes. Then she cooked another batch while he ate. They did that several times, trading off so they could both have hot pancakes.

When they were full, Drew drained the last of the coffee in the pot into their mugs and sat down again. They were at the table, sitting across from each other, and it seemed silly to Drew to just drink her coffee and ignore Orion.

"Do you have family in Laramie?" she questioned.

"No family anywhere."

No family at all seemed sad to Drew. Her brothers drove her up the wall at times, but what would she do without them? And without her sisters-in-law, and Judd's son, Petey, and Simon's daughters, Lisa and Rosie? Her nieces and nephew were very important to her. She never forgot their birthdays or failed to look for special gifts at Christmas.

"You're not from the Laramie area, are you?" she inquired.

"I was born in Sheridan. Moved to Laramie four years ago." Nick wasn't pleased with the small talk. His mind was centered on getting out of these mountains, not on the past. Besides, he avoided even thinking about his painful past; he certainly wasn't going to dredge it up for Drew LeBeau.

Drew wanted to keep the conversation going, as desultory as it was. Orion aroused her curiosity. He had a steely wall around himself, for some reason. Oh, he was no slouch in the holding-his-own department, and he'd let her know at every opportunity just how abidingly angry he was at being trapped out here.

But there had to be more to the man than anger. Maybe she only wanted there to be more, Drew mused, but she felt something unique with Nick Orion, and for some crazy reason she felt driven to find out what it meant.

She wasn't going to get the chance so soon, she realized when Orion stood up. "I'm going for a walk."

Drew cocked an eyebrow. "In the rain?" She received a mind-your-own-business look for her concern, which set her hair on end. "Arrogant jerk," she muttered as the back door closed behind Orion's exit.

Whether or not he was an arrogant jerk was moot at the moment. The man simply could not sit still and do nothing, and relaxing over coffee after breakfast was apparently impossible for him.

Lingering with her own coffee, Drew amused herself with her imagination. Visualizing Orion as a lover *was* amusing, wasn't it?

She delved deeper into the speculative fantasy, and found herself to be anything *but* amused. If Orion ever turned on the charm, it would take an incredible amount of self-control to remain detached. The man was sexy, damn him! Sexier than any man she'd ever known.

Drew took an oddly shaky breath. Thinking about Nick Orion and the bedroom as one entity was doing some very weird things to her. Unnerved, she got up and began clearing the table. That was the last thing she needed right now, to be attracted to a grouch like Orion!

The day passed with only the most necessary communication. Drew went to bed that night in a black mood. Orion had her stymied, and it was the most frustrating feeling she'd ever had to endure. They should have talked. He should have given her an opportunity to explain why she'd wanted him out here. Lying in the dark, Drew ardently prayed that someone would think of looking for them at the ranch.

And the blessed rain hadn't let up. All day Drew had kept a close eye on the weather, and while the intensity of rain fluctuated from heavy to merely misty, it had never completely stopped falling.

By dinner, Drew had wanted to scream at Orion, or at something. They'd eaten the makeshift meal with few words. He was slowly driving her crazy, and if they were out here for God knew how long, she wasn't sure what she might end up doing.

Drew stretched out her legs, seeking the same comfort she'd attained last night. The old bed felt lumpy, miserably uncomfortable. She was as cross as a she-bear with cubs, and she knew exactly who to blame for her mood.

How dare the man treat her so shabbily? Most of the time he looked right through her, and when he wasn't ignoring her, he was glaring at her.

He'd been clean-shaven this morning, Drew remembered, which meant that he had a few essentials with him, also. Like her flight bag, Orion's briefcase must be a carryall, so he wasn't so bad off. He had food, indoor plumbing and a good solid roof over his head. Not only that, he had a maid. Wasn't she doing all the cooking? Maybe she should suggest in the morning that if he wanted anything to eat, he could damn well cook it himself!

At least he wasn't sleeping any better than she was,

she thought, with a smug smile, as boot steps passed her door for the third time since she'd gone to bed. Orion was restless during the day and restless at night. Didn't he ever unwind?

Well, tonight she was wound just as tightly. She had been willing to make the best of things, Lord knew she'd tried. But with a thankless, odious person such as Orion to contend with, a saint would be pulling out her hair.

And none of the LeBeaus had ever been accused of saintliness.

Drew sighed. She had never thought it possible to be melancholy or depressed in this house. This was where she came when something got her down in town. What was getting her down now, though, was only a few walls away. Orion was a night prowler and an intruder, and it was maddening to have to face the fact that in spite of all his faults, he was the most searingly magnetic man she'd ever been around.

She hated him, she really did. He was rude and selfish and intolerant and petty. His dislike was a gift, something she should cherish. She should be rejoicing that he tried so hard to avoid her. She should...she should...

Tears seeped from her eyes, and Drew angrily brushed them away. Whatever it was that she *should* be doing, she was going to get up in the morning and carry on, the same as she'd done today.

But one thing was certain. When this was over, she was going to tell Nick Orion right to his face what a smug, self-centered, unforgiving jerk he was. Satisfied, at least, with that decision, Drew turned over and closed her eyes.

* * *

Nick's patience had long since died. Oddly enough, while patience was glaringly absent from his system, so was *im*patience. He felt strange, too restless to sleep, but not because of frustration. He felt…different.

With a pot of hot tea—his stomach had been protesting the chili he'd eaten for dinner—Nick sat at the kitchen table and listened to the absolute stillness, broken only by the gentle patter of rain on the roof. No telephone within reach was an incredible departure from routine. No one pestering him with questions, ideas, disputes or the dozens of other reasons requiring communication every minute of every hour, had been creating a void in his gut that felt as big as the Grand Canyon.

Tonight he still felt empty, but his system wasn't fighting inevitability quite so hard. His body was losing tension, his emotions, also. He was drinking tea in the middle of a rainy night, sitting in the kitchen of an impossibly isolated ranch house, and his worry about the situation was losing impetus. His denials of acceptance, too. He was here and there wasn't one blasted thing he could do about it. That's what was beginning to really sink in, that the whole thing was truly out of his hands.

Maybe he'd used up anger and resentment, he pondered. Despising Drew LeBeau had taken a lot of energy. He could actually think of her tonight without seeing red.

He had never let her explain the motivation behind her actions. It had something to do with this ranch, of course. Why else would she have wanted him here? She had tried to make amends, which he'd been refusing to acknowledge. He'd been hard on Drew, as cold and forbidding as one person could be with another.

Maybe he'd been a little too hard on her. Was his anger solely because of her rashness? He lived on a very strict regimen, by choice, and being dropped into such a completely opposite situation, where there was little to do and virtually no one to do it with, was deadly. Wasn't that the real cause of his frustration?

Nick took a swallow of tea. In this imperfect world, Drew LeBeau was probably no better or worse than anyone else. Everyone had their own little quirks, and she was obviously a responsible person most of the time. Flying for the Forest Service was a serious career. He knew what those pilots did, delivering people and supplies all over the country, risking their necks during forest fires.

Nick knew that he'd been more furious about Drew interrupting his work than endangering his life. But he also knew that George would make sure the company didn't slow down in his absence. No one was indispensable, not even Nick Orion.

He grinned wryly. Even Nick Orion was replaceable, which wasn't even close to the way he'd been living. His motor had operated at full throttle for years now, ever since...

His grin vanished, and he inhaled a long, unsteady breath. Mary...and little Katie...damn! He had too much time to think out here, to remember. Keeping the past locked deep in his own soul wasn't possible with nothing else to do, without ringing telephones and ceaseless work.

He'd nearly lost his mind when his wife and five-year-old daughter were killed in a highway accident just outside of Sheridan. He had been working for a developer, laying out lots, doing a little selling, and after the accident he hadn't gone to work at all. Not for a year. For nearly twelve months he'd bummed around and drank too much and suffered the agonies of hell.

But when his house—Mary's house—had been seized because he hadn't made the mortgage payments and his car had been repossessed and he had nothing left except a few boxes of personal possessions, he'd known what rock-bottom looked and felt like.

That's when he had left Sheridan. He managed to scrape up a few hundred bucks for an old beater of a car, and he drove off without a destination in mind. He ended up in Laramie, after a month of drifting and working odd jobs.

He'd known and understood only one field: land development. After finding a job at a gas station, which would barely feed and house him, he started looking for a piece of raw land that he could buy without a down payment. It hadn't been easy, but he'd finally met a man who had been willing to take a chance with his two hundred acres.

The rest was history. The first year had been a monumental struggle, the second a little easier. Then the company took off, and after only four years it was a respected and successful part of Wyoming.

Nick had learned one very important lesson during those four years: working was better than drinking for forgetting. He never touched alcohol anymore, and he filled his days and nights with work. It was definitely the best medicine for what ailed him.

But he'd never, ever dreamed that something like the situation he was in now would happen to him. Since he'd started the company, he hadn't had to deal with hours and hours of idleness, and he knew he hadn't been handling the forced confinement at all well.

The rain on the roof seeped into his thoughts. The tea was warming his insides. The house was quiet. One small light burned in the kitchen. An almost eerie peace seemed to be demanding recognition. He felt... different.

Nick got up and brought his mug to the sink. Maybe he could sleep now.

Drew did the avoiding the next day. If Orion was in the kitchen, she retreated to the living room. If he wandered in, she went to her bedroom. The storm was dissipating, but slowly, and in its wake the temperature was hovering in the fifties, keeping the house chilly and damp.

Around noon, with a feeble sun attempting to penetrate the heavy cloud cover, Drew left the house and set out for Black Creek. If it was passable, she intended to hike to the Hoskins ranch, to leave very early the next morning. After two days everyone in Laramie had to be frantic, and worrying about it was playing havoc with Drew's nervous system.

Orion was wreaking havoc on her nerves, too. He was a big man, and she couldn't pretend not to be aware of his every movement, even when she was in another room. He affected her as no man ever had, causing turmoil and a run of emotions she couldn't control—or understand—no matter how hard she tried.

Drew tramped through the saturated woods. Her feet were getting wet, as well as her clothing. She would be soaked through long before she got back to the house, but she had to see Black Creek to make a sensible decision on the hike.

Heavy, wet branches slapped at her, leaves and brush on the ground clung to her boots. Her light jacket wasn't sufficient protection against such weather, and she could only hope her effort wouldn't be rewarded with a cold, or worse.

Then, after an hour of pure misery, when she saw that Black Creek was a ten-foot-wide torrent of angry water, her spirit deflated to the point of despair. Spotting a stump, she sat down wearily. This avenue of rescue was impossible, and it had been her only hope. She stared broodingly at the rushing water. The creek's level would drop back to normal, but not for days. Runoff took time, and time was running out.

Disheartened, Drew forced herself back on her feet for the return trek. There was little point to sitting out here and wishing to God Nick Orion had never been born. Or, at the very least, had never moved to Laramie.

"Where in hell have you been?"

Orion was standing on the porch in a menacing stance, his face as dark as the darkest thundercloud.

"I beg your pardon," Drew said haughtily, mounting the stairs and whisking past him.

Nick followed her into the kitchen. "You might have said something before you disappeared. I didn't know *what* to think."

Drew turned with a cynical expression. "Don't tell me you were worried about me! You've been in and out right from the first. Have you told me even once what you were doing? Don't expect courtesy, Orion. Not from me. Maybe the other people you know enjoy your abysmal lack of humanity, but I find it repugnant!"

Whirling, Drew strode from the kitchen. She had to get out of her wet clothes, although what she was going

to cover her chilled body with while they dried was
bothering her. Muttering about Orion's unmitigated
gall, she began a search of the closets in each bedroom,
Orion's included. She was positive none of her own
things was here, but one of her brothers might have
left something.

Anything would do. An old shirt and a pair of jeans
would be great, although she would flounder in them.
Judd and Simon were twice her size, but she could tie
their clothes in place, if she had to.

There was nothing. The closets were empty, just as
she'd known they were. She would have to settle for a
blanket, and if Orion didn't like it, tough!

Shivering, Drew went to her own bedroom and
peeled off her wet clothes. Yanking a blanket off the
bed, she draped it around herself. Her slacks had a belt,
and she finally got the thing strapped around herself
and the blanket so that she was covered from neck to
ankles.

Her boots were soggy, but she had a pair of dry
socks in her flight bag and she pulled them on.

Then she carried the wet clothing to the bathroom,
figuring she might as well wash the garments since they
had to be dried, anyway. She had previously rinsed out
underthings and socks, and with her and Orion's
nightly showers, the bar of soap was getting dangerously small.

Drew sighed. Supplies were bound to run out. The
house hadn't been stocked for a long siege. Actually,
she and Orion were incredibly fortunate that it had been
stocked at all. Didn't he realize that? Didn't he ever
stop to think how bad things *could* have been?

The man was an ingrate, the most insensitive clod

she had ever met. Good-looking? Sexy? So damned what!

With the clothing cleaner than it had been, Drew eyed the shower rod. Orion would probably be ticked off about that, too. She had used the chair in her bedroom for her small articles, but her slacks and shirt needed more space.

"Orion can stew in his own nasty juices," Drew mumbled while adorning the shower rod. Anything she did riled him in one way or another, so why should she worry about what he might think about this?

With that chore out of the way, Drew thought of another one. A pleasant one. She would build a fire in the fireplace, and she would sit in front of it and get warm, no matter which room Orion decided to use for his intolerable pacing.

Determined to follow through, Drew strode down the hall to the living room. She stopped dead in her tracks in the doorway: a fire was already burning. Orion was on his knees in front of the hearth, stirring the blazing logs with the old cast-iron poker.

Uncertain again, Drew stood there and stared. Orion was just full of surprises, wasn't he? Had he built the fire because of her?

Fat chance! Just because she'd been dripping water and shivering, Orion had not suddenly turned into a nice guy.

Nick sensed Drew behind him, and he glanced over his shoulder to where she was standing in the doorway. Startled by the blue blanket, he gave it a quick once-over. She looked small in its generous folds, defenseless. Which was a crock. Drew LeBeau might be small, but she was far from defenseless.

Last night he'd decided to let up on her, and today

she'd gone off without a word and scared the stuffing out of him. So much for good intentions.

But he'd seen how wet and cold she was, and a fire was a good idea, in any case. He should have thought of one yesterday. It might have made the day a little less stressful.

"What are you waiting for? Come on over and soak up some of this heat."

Orion had just about the same amount of charm as a case of the measles, Drew thought dryly. She needn't have wasted any time speculating on his irresistibility, should he suddenly see her as a woman.

He moved over about a foot, giving her plenty of room to sit in front of the fire. Orion hovering within touching distance was totally immaterial. Drew gravitated toward the flames, only slightly less eager than a mindless moth, and remembered to adjust the blanket for her descent to the floor just on the edge of decency.

Nick caught the flash of skin out of the corner of his eye and frowned at the electrical current zapping his body. It hadn't been *that* long since he'd been with a woman, had it?

He sat back on his heels. It had been long enough that he couldn't remember the woman's face. There'd been how many, two, three women since his move to Laramie? No one important. Never anyone important. His energy went into his work, not into chasing women.

But maybe he'd been remiss in that area of his life. If he was finding Drew LeBeau interesting, he'd definitely done something wrong.

She held out her hands to the heat, splaying her fingers, absorbing the warmth with an almost purring pleasure. Even Orion's grating presence couldn't ruin this moment, she thought with a small smile.

"Where'd you go?"

He was looking at her, and there was something just a shade possessive in his eyes. The male ego was incredible, Drew thought. Orion disliked her, resented her, and more than likely was planning to raise hell with her pilot's license. But because she was a mere woman and he was a big, strong man, he believed he had the right to stick his nose into her business.

The age-old battle between the sexes had always left Drew cold. She'd had her own battles to fight, and they had been much closer to home. Outside her own family, she'd been fairly dealt with, she felt. Education, training and a subsequent job, a darned good job, had progressed without gender discrimination.

But with Judd and Simon for brothers, she knew all about discrimination. And about male egos, and how protective a man could appear to be, when all he was really doing was telling a woman how high to jump.

Drew mulled it over. With Orion's bigger-than-life ego, he'd probably insist on trying to cross Black Creek, never mind the danger. Her brothers would, she was certain. Her brothers wouldn't even *see* the danger, for that matter.

And neither would Nick Orion.

Nope, she wasn't going to have that on her conscience, not along with what she was already carrying.

"I just needed a good long walk," she lied. "I'm not used to being cooped up."

"A long walk in the rain?"

The man was too, too clever, turning her very own question back on her, the one she'd used when he'd announced a walk in the less than balmy weather.

"That's rather funny, coming from a man who can't sit still for five minutes at a time."

"I don't see you laughing."

"I don't think either of us sees the situation as amusing."

Nick was feeling an odd mellowness. More than the heat from the fireplace was warming his bones. The blanket-wrapped woman sitting beside him was causing a familiar—if rarely heeded, anymore—reaction. It was purely physical, of course. A man and a woman alone, the woman obviously naked under a faded old blanket, a fireplace radiating heat, the isolation. It was starting to click into place, each separate factor nestling against all of the others.

And Drew LeBeau wasn't at all hard on the eyes. Her short blond hair was still damp, curling around her pretty face in wispy tentacles. Her skin had a rosy glow, a reflected color from the flickering flames. Her mouth was drawing his gaze, again and again.

Nick cleared his throat and forced his eyes to the fire. He gave it a good poke and sent a shower of sparks up the chimney. "So...what direction did you walk in?"

"Direction?" Drew sent him a quick glance. "What difference does that make?"

"I've done a little walking myself, you know. I was hoping to run across someone, a cabin, maybe."

Drew shook her head. "There aren't any cabins, not for two thousand acres, at least. You should know that. You're on LeBeau land, remember? And why on earth wouldn't I have told you if someone was nearby? Do you think I like being stranded out here any better than you do?"

Five

Nick thought of saying something about her "devious" mind again, but he didn't want her to get all bent out of shape. Sitting here together was almost pleasant, and the warm liquidity of his own system was tugging at emotions. Drew was getting prettier and more desirable by the minute, and he couldn't stop himself from wondering how she might receive a pass.

He dampened his lips with his tongue and tried to concentrate on her question. His body's increasingly demanding need for sex was alien to his nature. He didn't jump a woman just because he was alone with one. He rarely made passes at women he really liked, so what was going on in his brain now?

"Whether you enjoy being out here any more than I do really isn't the problem, is it?" he finally managed to get out, huskily.

"What?" He'd taken so long to answer, Drew had

practically forgotten the topic. "Oh, yes. Well, our biggest problem is getting back to Laramie," she replied, wondering about the queer hoarseness in Orion's voice.

"Yes. Getting back to Laramie." Nick had another problem to deal with, and if Drew happened to glance at his lap, she would know exactly what it was. He shifted his position so that he could raise his left thigh and conceal what was becoming much too obvious.

That blanket was driving him nuts. "Uh…where are your clothes?"

Orion was acting weird. He was talking to her, which was an enormous deviation from what she'd gotten from him so far, but not only that, he was giving off some very disturbing vibes. Drew gave him a furtive but intense sidelong look. He was sitting funny, sort of crooked, and his face seemed to be flushed.

Hers had to be flushed, too, though. The fireplace was throwing off massive waves of heat. In fact, she was actually getting a little *too* warm.

"My clothes are hanging over the shower rod." Drew waited for the inevitable snide remark, and when she didn't hear one, she gave Orion a direct stare and a bluntly put, "What's going on?"

"Nothing's going on."

"How come you're talking to me?"

Nick winced. "I've been a jerk, haven't I?"

"You won't get an argument from me on that," Drew drawled.

Nick smiled, first at the dancing flames in the fireplace and then, with a turn of his head, at Drew. Her heart nearly stopped beating. The man *could* smile, and exceedingly well, too. His eyes—Lord, what beautiful eyes! His mouth, his whole face. He was gorgeous, exciting, wonderful to look at, so handsome she could barely breathe.

Drew's mouth was suddenly desert-dry. Orion had to know the power of that smile. He had to know that her heart had not only resumed beating, it was running wild. As for feeling flushed, her face had to have caught fire!

Nick edged close enough to lean forward and touch her hair. Drew couldn't move. The blood was racing through her body with the speed of light. This shouldn't be happening, but she couldn't lift a finger to prevent it.

She watched his eyes roam her features, as though he was absorbing each and every nuance of her face, while his fingers gently brushed through her hair. "Nice," he murmured. "Very nice."

When had she become nice? And why couldn't she leap and run?

Her own senses were betraying her. Orion's touch was mesmerizing, zooming through her body and creating an overwhelming weakness. She knew what was happening; Orion was making a pass! His about-face was astounding, but no more so than her own reactions.

She could still think, and the questions were piling up. She'd never been promiscuous, and making love with a man she barely knew was unheard of. Especially a man like Nick Orion. Was she mad?

She was something, Drew knew, although what that might be wasn't to be grasped. Not at the moment, anyway. And maybe it wasn't all that important. Maybe the hot, steamy sensations taunting and daring her were all that mattered.

Nick inched closer still. Drew was really very beautiful with her big green eyes and sensual mouth. Why hadn't he seen that before? His heart was knocking against his rib cage, and he knew he was about to do something he wouldn't have thought possible only an hour ago.

His mouth slowly moved nearer to hers, until he could smell the mint of toothpaste on her breath. "Drew...I'm sorry about the last few days," he whispered. "Can you forgive me?"

Sins and forgiveness were flicked away with one small nod of Drew's head. He hadn't done anything so terrible. "Do you forgive me?" she asked breathlessly.

"For causing this moment?" There was that fabulous smile again, implying to Drew that she'd done something wonderful and he'd known it all along. Her insides dissolved into pure mush.

Nick threaded his fingers into her hair and clasped the back of her head. "You smell so good," he whispered, and fitted his lips to hers.

Her eyes closed in a wave of utter bliss. Nick's mouth was warm and sure and causing her very skin to tingle. His lips worked hers apart, a very small task when she was so willing, and settled into a deeper, more drugging kiss.

She moved her hands up his shoulders and around his neck. Vaguely she was aware of being lowered to the floor, but it was done so slowly and so gently, and with so many heated sensations darting around in her body, she made no protest.

When she opened her eyes again, it was to see Nick looking down at her. They were lying on the carpet, only a few feet from the hearth, she on her back, him leaning over her. His lips were wet, his eyes glazed. "You're a very special lady," he whispered raggedly.

His mouth came down again, claiming hers in another mind-spinning kiss.

He was breathing hard, as worked up as she was, Drew realized. His tongue was in her mouth, and his hand was roving. She couldn't seem to say no. In spite of an immense bank of reservations in the back of her mind, she didn't have the willpower to tell him to stop.

She felt the blanket slipping, being pushed out of his way. Somehow he'd undone her belt, and after that the blanket was of small import. His hand skimmed her bare skin, lighting fires of response wherever it reached, her thighs, her back, her behind.

And her breasts. The kisses blended from one to the next, and he caressed her breasts, holding their weight, teasing her nipples. She was sinking deeper and deeper into her own desire. It had been ignited by Orion, but belonged only to her, nonetheless. She'd seen and admitted a certain fascination with the man before this, and hadn't she fantasized about how he'd behave in bed?

Drew put those thoughts aside. Thinking was becoming difficult, anyway, and tormenting herself with memories of the past few days, when she didn't have the strength to halt either Orion or herself, was silly. She was a big girl, she told herself, and Nick Orion was the most incredibly thrilling man she'd ever met.

He broke the chain of kisses, to trail his lips down to her throat. Drew made a small gasping sound when his mouth moved lower and captured the crest of her breast. His tongue flicked while he gently sucked, and Drew's desire exploded into blinding, mindless passion.

Her fingers clutched at his shoulders, and at his hair. "Nick...Nick..."

"I'm here, baby. I'm right here."

He was trying to struggle out of his clothes without losing anything in the process. This was one passionate, excited lady, and pleasing her was going to please him. A lot.

Naked, he bent his head and kissed her beautiful swollen lips. His insides were oozy with tenderness. Any woman who made a man feel as he did deserved every consideration. He smoothed the blanket beneath her, making sure she was comfortable, and kissed her again and again.

She was gasping for breath. Her hands kept traveling his body, searchingly, with obvious agitation. Her tongue found his, her mouth clung to his.

His hand slid down her stomach. She was hot and wet and ready for him, but he explored and stroked through several more long kisses.

He had no protection with him. Who would have guessed he would need it the morning he left Laramie? But there was very little with the power to stop him right now. An earthquake, maybe. He was going to have his own little earthquake, and so was Drew LeBeau. He'd make sure she was satisfied, she could count on that courtesy.

Drew was so dazed she wasn't seeing straight. The room seemed to be spinning like a top. Certainly the flames in the fireplace were leaping higher and higher, as though fanned by an unseen hand.

It wasn't Orion's hand, because his was between her legs and doing incredible things to her.

She clasped him harder. "Nick..."

He heard the plea in his name, the need. He was almost out of control himself, despite an inordinate amount of determination to stay calm until the right moment. This was wild. *Drew* was wild. She had worked him up without meaning to, but damn, she was something!

Drew's nails dug into his back as he slid into her. "Oh, Nick," she whispered, so internally shaken she didn't know if she was in Wyoming or China. She adored Nick Orion with every fiber of her being. She breathed for Nick Orion. She *lived* for Nick Orion.

She'd been born for this moment, and this beautiful, precious moment was why no other man had ever been quite right for her.

His body rocked on hers, loved hers, and she returned every movement, every caress. For long, intensely meaningful minutes they moved as one. Drew's hands glided over his broad back and then downward to the tight masculine muscles in his buttocks.

Words formed in her mind, ragged-edged phrases that didn't quite reach her lips. Instead, she emitted small moans and gasps and vocalized attempts to catch a breath of air.

It all came together in a searing rush, emotion, pleasure, sheer, exquisitely sweet rapture. Drew's eyes filled with tears as the spasms went on and on, meeting and matching Nick's ardor.

There was no doubting she'd given him pleasure, just as he'd given her. Nick had quietened. His head was down, lying beside hers. Drew's hands moved dreamily over his sweat-slick back. They just lay there, neither speaking, for a long time.

"I think the fire's dying," Drew said softly, eyeing the diminished flames in the fireplace. She wanted to look into Nick's eyes, to see what he was thinking now.

He raised his head to glance at the fire. "Yeah, it is. Let me fix it."

He moved away from her, and she was instantly cold. She had to get up and go to the bathroom, she knew. They had dared fate today, risking pregnancy, and that thought alone was enough to start her teeth chattering.

Drawing the blanket up around herself, Drew scurried off.

Nick sent her a guilty glance, and the second she was out of sight he grabbed his clothes and yanked them on. He stood there, looking down at the dying fire and rubbing his mouth. What had he done? Drew LeBeau wasn't a woman for him to be fooling around with. He was doing business with her brothers!

This wasn't like him, not at *all* like him. When had he ever become so hungry for a woman that he'd let himself get so swept away?

Never, that's when. Not since high school, when he'd fallen so hard for Mary.

And whatever this was with Drew LeBeau, it wasn't anything like he'd had with Mary. She had been sweet clear through, soft-spoken, always giving of her time and energy. Drew LeBeau had skin an inch thick and very little tact. She would probably slug it out with anyone, himself included, at the drop of a hat.

So…what did he do now? What was Drew going to expect from this little encounter?

What sort of woman was she? This wouldn't make a tinker's damn to some gals. There were women who lived as casually as some men did, and a roll around the floor wouldn't mean anything even remotely serious to them.

The knot in his gut told Nick that Drew wasn't in that category. He didn't know *how* he knew, but he was positive that he'd opened up one enormous can of worms today.

The blanket didn't seem adequate now. After such beautiful lovemaking, Drew yearned for something pretty and feminine to put on. The lavender silk robe hanging in her closet at home would be perfect, but wishing for that robe was like wishing for the stars.

Drew groped through the towel and bathroom-supplies cupboard, not content to give up and return to Nick wearing the blanket. Her slacks and sweatshirt were still dripping water from the shower rod, but wouldn't a big towel be just a tad better than this ratty old blanket?

There wasn't anything big enough. Or good enough, for that matter. Sighing, Drew reached for her small bag of cosmetics. At least she could dab on a little makeup. She wanted to be pretty for Nick. His fabulous blue eyes would light up, she was positive. He would see that she had put on a hint of lipstick and some mascara for him, that she'd done what she could to look special for him.

And then he would take her in his arms again, and they would laugh together about how they'd met. It was really very funny, when she thought about it. Her detouring without his permission, him so pushed out of shape and furious. Oh, yes, looking back at it all, it was like one of those situation comedies on TV. Even their rough landing, which was extremely serious busi-ness, had a comedic feel to it now.

She was gloriously, unbelievably happy, that's why everything seemed funny or wonderful.

After all, she had never really been in love before.

* * *

Nick wished he could just disappear, evaporate, or shrink into something invisible to the naked eye. He was a jerk, a damned fool, the kind of man he'd always laughed at, a guy who thought with his zipper.

It had never happened to him before. Even with Mary, when he'd been young and full of vinegar, he hadn't been as lecherous as he'd just been with Drew. Besides, the physical urges he'd felt with Mary had been a result of loving her so much.

He didn't love Drew LeBeau. Hell, he wasn't sure if he even liked her. He sure hadn't thought very much of her before she had suddenly become so tantalizing, which was shocking enough, now that his libido had settled down, to send him into outer space.

"Nick?"

He turned, smiling rather sickishly. "Drew, I think we need to...talk."

"Why, yes, I think so, too." She was so giddy, she felt as if she were floating inches off the floor. He'd gotten dressed, she noticed, although his shirt was buttoned funny. She laughed. "Here, let me fix this."

Nick stood there and let her rearrange his buttons and buttonholes. She smelled so good, just as he'd told her. And he saw the extra pink on her lips and the darkness of her long lashes. This was no trivial experience for Drew LeBeau. His heart began pumping too hard again, this time from regret and guilt.

He put his hands on her shoulders, intending to soothe her throughout his confession, through what could only be a painful time for her. But she smiled softly and leaned into him, bringing her arms up around his neck.

"Oh, Nick, I can't tell you...I mean, *how* can I tell

you?'' Her laughter was fuzzy, a husky run of notes that made Nick feel lightheaded.

She was so warm and female, so wonderfully uninhibited. He was only human, and he'd lacked female companionship for a long time, even if he hadn't realized it until very, very recently.

His conscience began receding, crawling behind a renewal of desire, taking reason with it, and caution and good sense. His hands slid from her shoulders to her back and downward, and as if they had a mind of their own, they brought her forward until the two of them were pressed tightly together.

He could feel her heartbeat, hear his own. A totally male voice somewhere in his brain told him that she was making him want her again, that the first time might have been his doing, but this was *her* doing.

She kissed him. On tiptoe, with her arms wrapped around his neck, she kissed him on the mouth, tenderly mating their lips, wetting his with the tip of her tongue. Passion rocketed through Nick again.

These sudden, overwhelming surges of excitement were something to wonder about after lying dormant for so long. Even dazed with desire again, Nick knew he would wonder in days to come, about himself, about Drew, about why he couldn't grab hold of his own impulses and knock them out of his system.

He'd told her she was a special woman and she was. Chemistry wasn't controllable between two people; it was either present or it wasn't. That was the only logic in today's misbehavior, Nick thought vaguely, and Drew had to know that as well as him.

They were so alone out here, and she was so female and eager. His hands slipped beneath the blanket and found bare, warm, silken skin. They were adults, and who were they harming? he asked himself. He closed his eyes and sank into the kiss.

After a few breathless moments, Drew whispered raggedly, "Oh, Nick." Emotionally committed to this man, her hands moved restlessly on his chest. His eyes were smoky with desire, reflecting her own feelings. "How did this happen?" she whispered.

"Kismet?"

Her eyes searched his. "I've never…" A fingertip on her lips stopped a confession of feelings never before experienced. Even that cautioning contact felt sensual to her and she moved her lips against his finger.

The electricity between them seemed to be bouncing off the walls. Nick's heart was jumping around, his blood pressure soaring. It was only circumstances, he told himself. The isolation. Maybe even the anger this whole thing had started with. Volatile emotions, *raw* emotions. Maybe making love like this was only a natural conclusion to their explosive relationship.

Whatever, walking away right now would be impossible. He slowly drew the blanket away from her shoulders and let it drop to the floor. Her cheeks got pinker, but she stood there and let him look at her naked body. "You are beautiful," he whispered hoarsely.

She was. Her breasts were full and crested by rose-tinted nipples. Below her bosom, her figure dipped to a tiny waistline, then flared again at her hips. There were tan lines on her skin, areas of paleness, with her legs the darkest of all.

There was sweet ecstasy in Drew's system, in every cell, every nerve, every ounce of her flesh and blood. She had never let a man look at her so, with his eyes dark and glittering. She was giving Nick Orion all of herself, she knew, holding nothing back, a dangerous game for a woman to be playing with a man she barely knew.

But her feelings couldn't be only one-sided. There was very little of her normal fighting spirit in her body right now, but she would still debate that point with anyone. They were too much in tune for her to be the only one thinking serious thoughts.

And if Nick couldn't seem to talk about it, she understood that, too,. He was basically a reticent man, but even silent people eventually opened up. He would speak his feelings in his own good time.

Besides, talking wasn't all that important to her right now, either. She felt glowingly, achingly alive, bursting with feelings she had only previously touched upon. They weren't merely trapped out here; they were so fortunate, the concept was mind-boggling. With any luck at all, they would be alone for days yet.

Drew's glance flicked to the fireplace. Nick hadn't rekindled the fire as he'd promised. The room was rapidly chilling and there were several good beds in the house. She smiled. "Your room or mine?"

Nick's heart took a strange flip. He should stop this right now. Not that putting a damper on things would alleviate his first offense, but making love again would immutably compound the sin.

He wanted her. He was hard and unreasonably aroused. He'd never been faced with a decision of this nature before, and he knew, even while mulling it over, that his baser urges were going to win the battle. It was because of Drew, herself. She wanted what he did. If there was even a smidgen of doubt on her pretty face, a hint of reluctance in her radiant green eyes, he would back off.

But there was no doubt or reluctance anywhere in sight.

With a wry expression, Nick bent over and scooped her off the floor and up into his arms. She laughed low and seductively and hugged his neck during the short walk to her room.

Nick laid her on the bed and stood up to undress. She scooted under the blankets, then watched him, her eyes following his every movement, deep green and expectant.

His heart was pounding almost violently. He tossed his shirt and opened his jeans.

Drew dampened her suddenly dry lips. There was a sense of unreality about the scene, but it was also the most real thing she'd ever been a part of. Her few past experiences with men paled by comparison. She felt like laughing and crying, both at the same time, a spillage of unleashed, unfamiliar emotions. While he shed his jeans, Drew slid back a corner of the blankets, making a place in her bed for him.

He crawled in and covered the top of her body with his, leaning over her, immediately initiating a long, hungry kiss. His hand moved beneath the blankets while his tongue explored her mouth. In mere seconds she was gasping with a massive onslaught of physical desire. No man had ever made her want so much, crave so much.

Within the blurred passages of her brain, she suspected no other man ever would. Nick Orion was her mate, and being the sort of woman she was, he would forever be her *only* mate. The knowledge was extremely satisfying.

It was the only pocket of satisfaction in her entire body. Nick was making her whimper with unrestrained longing. The blankets had been thrown back. His mouth was on her breast, his hand between her thighs. She reached for the magical maleness at the base of his tight belly, and reveled in the sensation of holding it in her hand.

"That's good," he whispered.

"I like touching you."

"I like it, too."

They both liked it. Just as they both liked how he was touching her. It was what made a particular couple special, Drew thought dreamily. The two people involved functioned on the same wavelength.

She closed her eyes for another kiss, sinking deeper into the pillow, becoming one with Nick and the bed. His fingertips skimmed her skin and the secrets of her body, igniting fires, increasing the depth of her hunger for him.

"You're wonderful," he whispered. His hands were hot and becoming greedy. Hers were, too. She was no longer content just to hold the weight of his manhood, and began to stroke and fondle.

Their bodies were becoming dewy with perspiration and neither seemed able to lie still. Nick threw a leg over hers, which eliminated any more of her stroking. But the adjustment aligned them in a tantalizingly intimate way. Drew shifted beneath him, aligning everything a little more precisely. She released a long "Ohhh" of intense pleasure. "Do it," she whispered.

He was ready to "do it," too, but she needed one small reminder. "We have nothing for protection, unless you're on the Pill."

"No...I...no."

"Don't worry about it. I'll withdraw."

That made sense to her, although she'd only heard

a few references to that particular birth-control technique. Stopping altogether wasn't an option, right at the moment, so she was willing to do anything Nick might suggest.

It all seemed obscure anyway, so unlikely. What were the odds of pregnancy the first—*second*—time one made love with a man? It could be her fertile time, she didn't keep track of such things, but out of a twenty-eight-day cycle, chances of today being the day weren't very probable.

Of course...if they were out here for an indefinite period of time...?

"Yes," she whispered, not even positive of what she was agreeing to.

Nick eased into her and then nearly choked on the blinding rush of pleasure he felt. Her body was tight and hot, responding to his invasion with a squeezing of muscles that nearly undid him. He put his head down and didn't move anything. "Give me a minute," he rasped.

She caressed his sweat-smooth back and closed her eyes. She was breathing erratically, her heart thumping unmercifully, her lower parts in flames. The intimate moment seemed extremely meaningful to Drew, and she thought about living out the rest of her life with Nick Orion. About being in his bed and in his arms every night for years to come.

He raised his head and looked into her eyes. She smiled, but his gaze had moved elsewhere. She wondered if he wasn't gritting his teeth, and if so, why?

His movements began very slowly and without much vigor. Perhaps he was tired, she mused, although only a few minutes ago he hadn't shown the slightest sign of exhaustion.

And then she understood, because he was moving very fast and going very deep, clutching at her, dropping kisses wherever they landed. Her whole system reacted. She rubbed his back and buttocks, and she bucked and writhed beneath him, matching his increasingly agitated thrusts with her own.

In the end there was no withdrawal. They reached simultaneous climaxes, moaning and gasping and breathing noisily enough to wake the dead.

A lethargy such as Drew had never felt before came upon her then. Her bones were gone, she was certain, melted down into something soft and elastic. Her eyelids drooped. She wanted to sleep and sleep.

She barely felt him move away and curl around her, and a flickering of eyelashes allowed just enough vision for her to note that the room was getting dimmer. The sun was going down.

She yawned and fell into a deep sleep.

Nick awoke to a pitch-black room. Drew was dead to the world beside him. Anxiety struck him hard and fast, followed closely by regret. Deliberately he eased away from the warm, pliant body tangled with his, and relaxed a little only when he was no longer touching Drew.

What comes next, Orion? he asked himself sardonically. He didn't want a long-term involvement. He was a man who found tremendous satisfaction in his work. This perplexing interlude had been great, but it was still only a pause in the normal routines of his life. Somehow he had to make Drew understand that without hurting her in the process.

Nick frowned in the dark. Women's feelings and reactions were a mystery to him, but every man who'd ever had even the most rudimentary connection to a woman knew that the female mind saw things differently than men did. Even Mary had surprised him at times with a completely erroneous interpretation of something he'd said or done. Talking to Drew about today wasn't going to be a simple matter.

It had to be done, though, and the sooner the better, before something else happened and the two of them got in any deeper than they already were.

Nick began to ease off the bed, moving very cautiously so Drew wouldn't be disturbed. He would finish the night in his own bed and initiate that crucial conversation first thing in the morning.

Dawn was just beginning to lighten the sky when Nick awoke, ravenously hungry. They had skipped supper last night, and his stomach was putting up a squawk of protest. He got out of bed, pulled on his clothes and tiptoed to the kitchen. In the gray morning light, his decision to talk to Drew wasn't quite so well defined as it had been in the dark last night. It was going to be a tough proposition, one he wasn't looking forward to.

Nick put on a pot of coffee to brew and went to the cabinet for the pancake mix. Then, holding the tin, he narrowed his eyes and cocked his head. Motor noises! Someone was getting very close!

Dropping everything, he raced through the house to the front door. He breathed a gigantic sigh of relief. Three vehicles, one of which belonged to George Hollister, drove up and stopped. Men poured out of the vehicles.

Nick hesitated. Drew was on his conscience. He saw

her brothers, both of them, getting out, seeing him, waving and calling to him.

There would be no discussion this morning between him and Drew, not with the house full of people.

And maybe it was best. What could he ever say to make what he'd done acceptable?

Six

"**D**rew? Wake·up, honey!"

The voice boomed throughout the house, bringing Drew wide-awake and upright in bed. "Judd!" she shrieked, and was halfway out of bed before she remembered her nudity. "Oh, my Lord," she whispered frantically. "Don't come in, Judd! I'll be out in a minute."

Where was Nick? Her bedroom door was closed, thank goodness, but when had he left her room?

The sound of other voices, men's voices, reached Drew's ears. Judd hadn't come alone. Simon was no doubt with him, and who else? The voices were varied, several talking at once, evidence of more than a few people congregating in the ranch house.

Drew grabbed a blanket and hugged it around herself. She cautiously opened the door and peeked down the hall. Nick's bedroom door was wide open, and she could see that the room was empty.

Quickly she ducked into the hall and ran to the bathroom. The clothes hanging from the shower rod were dry enough, she decided, and she began to scramble into them. Her heart was beating unusually hard. The men's voices—from the living room she was sure—created a scene of camaraderie and relief in her mind. Some backslapping was going on, some laughter. Clearly, the rescuers were elated to have finally located Drew LeBeau and Nick Orion.

Drew splashed water on her face and hurriedly brushed her teeth. She was shaking, and the trembling alarmed her.

Something was alarming her, at any rate. Was it Nick? When had he left her bed? And why? Where had he been when Judd and Simon arrived? She had slept so soundly, and what had gone on in the night?

Seeing Nick seemed all-important, crucial. Last night had been the most moving experience of her life. She adored the man, loved him with all of her heart and soul. And she wanted to stand by his side and by proximity alone announce to everyone that something wonderful had happened at Black Creek Ranch.

The minutes she took to put on makeup seemed to drag, but she couldn't go out among those men and stand next to Nick without looking her best. The trembling wouldn't abate. Her insides were jumping around as much as her hands.

"Drew? Whatcha doing in there so long?"

It was Judd again. "Another minute," she called.

"Are you okay?"

"I'm fine."

"Well, hurry it up. We're all anxious to get a look at you."

A *probing* look, Drew was certain. Everyone was bound to be curious. Was Nick explaining what had happened?

Drew's stomach turned over. Explanations weren't going to be easy, not to her brothers, at least. When it came out that she had flown Nick to the ranch without his permission, Judd and Simon would probably puff up like angry toads.

"Darn," she muttered, vigorously brushing her hair. She didn't want a scene with her brothers, but they were crusty, outspoken men and neither would understand their sister's motives in bringing Nick Orion out here. Not if she explained until she was blue in the face.

She was as presentable as possible, under the circumstances, Drew finally decided. Squaring her shoulders, she left the bathroom and headed for the living room.

"Drew!" She received a big hug from Judd.

"Little sister!" She received a big hug from Simon.

And then the others crowded around, a man from the sheriff's department, a pilot she knew, and a friend who worked for the Forest Service. She smiled and assured them all that she was fine, that she hadn't been injured in the forced landing. She began to answer questions, from the pilot, in particular. Technical questions.

Her eyes swept beyond the men around her and found Nick talking to two men. Strangers to her. Not to Nick, apparently. He seemed engrossed in the conversation, although there was no way he could have missed her entrance.

But he didn't look at her. There was nothing from

him, no smile sent across the room, no sign whatsoever that she was standing no more than ten feet away.

Drew's heart began pounding. Why wouldn't he acknowledge her presence?

One of the men in Nick's group walked over. "I'm George Hollister, Drew." He held out his right hand. "Nick told us how your quick thinking saved the day. I, for one, want to thank you."

Drew stared at the man, then took his hand with a feeling of numbness. He spoke again. "Nick doesn't normally change his daily schedule, which was why no one thought to look up here right away."

Judd dropped an arm around his sister's shoulders. "Simon and I were talking last night, and it occurred to us that Nick might have wanted another look at the ranch."

She was getting the picture. Nick, apparently, had told everyone that coming here had been *his* idea.

Drew peered around the men crowding her, to see Nick again. He was still involved, still standing in a position that precluded direct eye contact.

He was doing it on purpose! He wasn't looking at her because he didn't *want* to look at her.

She was so stunned she nearly blacked out. Last night...oh, God, last night...

She couldn't think and she didn't dare cry, although her eyes had started burning like two live coals. He had used her, damn him, *used* her!

And what did that make her? There were names for women who made love with a man at his first hint of interest, ugly names.

But she had to be mistaken, she *had* to! If only they were alone. If only she could talk to him privately.

He wasn't going to give her the chance, she realized

dully as the rescuers started making motions to leave. Nick was almost the first one through the door, and he was already carrying his briefcase. She vaguely assimilated snatches of conversation: a mechanic and pilot would be sent up to repair and fly the helicopter back to Laramie.

"My flight bag," she said huskily.

"I'll get it," Simon volunteered.

"No, I'll do it. I've got a few things scattered around."

She started from the room, but hesitated when Judd went to the front door and called out, "See you guys back in town."

Drew heard Nick's reply. "We'll get together sometime in the next few days, Judd. Thanks again."

There was nothing from Nick to her, no word of comfort, no hint of another meeting. He'd had his fun—my God, was that really all last night had meant to him?—and it was over.

Disbelief mingled with the nausea in her system. She had never been betrayed by a man before, and it was the most paralyzing sensation she had ever experienced. Her brain wasn't functioning beyond reactions to the pain she was feeling.

Somehow she stumbled through the next few minutes, gathering up the articles that belonged in her flight bag. She was leaving her bed in a mess, but she didn't care. Avoiding even looking at the sheets and blankets strewn across the mattress, she hurried back to the living room.

Getting out of here suddenly seemed imperative. Once away from the ranch, she might be able to breathe without choking.

"I'm ready," she announced.

Judd gave her a quizzical look. "Are you sure you're all right?"

He was the only one still in the house, waiting for her, obviously. Drew moved to the front door and saw two vehicles, Judd's Wagoneer and a Blazer with a sheriff's-department insignia on the door.

Nick, George Hollister and the man she hadn't met had apparently left in yet another vehicle. The LeBeaus got in Judd's Wagoneer and the pilot rode with the deputy.

Drew had insisted on the backseat, and she tried to sit straight and not appear as bruised as she felt. Simon again related how he and Judd had decided to check the ranch, while Judd maneuvered the snaky mountain roads, with Judd chiming in with his point of view and Drew making appropriate—she hoped—comments.

Her contribution wasn't good enough, apparently, because Simon turned in his seat to give her a long look. "Are you sure you're okay? You're awfully quiet."

Judd threw a frown over his shoulder. "What kind of man is Orion?"

Drew swallowed. "What do you mean, what kind of man is he?"

"Just what I said. You two were alone up there for three nights. Did he try something?"

That's when the hatred began, the awful heat of fury and bitterness. If she told her brothers that, yes, Orion had tried something, they would be furious. She could start a war of open hostility right now, and Judd and Simon might get so outraged they would refuse to do business with Nick.

But selling the ranch no longer had any meaning. In fact, would she ever go back, even if it stayed in the family? The thought of walking into that house and looking at the hearth, of using her own bedroom again, of being so close to memory, was repellant.

Besides, she couldn't tell anyone what a fool she'd been, especially her brothers.

Simon was stoically staring, waiting for an answer. "Orion is a horse's behind," she said dully. "But he didn't do anything I couldn't handle."

Simon grinned and faced front again. "She'd knock any man's block clean off if he tried something funny," he remarked to Judd. The brothers chuckled, and Drew stared broodingly out of the side window behind them.

She would never forget this, never! And if the opportunity ever arose to pay Nick Orion back, she would take it.

The *Laramie Daily News* requested an interview, which Drew refused. Nick had no such reservations, she decided, because she read *his* interview in the morning paper the next day. It made her sick to her stomach.

Without Drew LeBeau's command of the situation, we could have been killed or, at the very least, seriously injured.

Did he think that omitting her sin of taking him to the ranch without his permission could atone for what he'd done? Nick's digression was infuriating, the way a pat on the head would be after kicking a dog.

Maybe he saw it as compensation for the excitement she had given him.

That thought made her sicker still.

The following Monday morning Drew walked into her supervisor's office. "May I have a few minutes?"

she asked Larry Harmon.

"Sure. Close the door and sit down."

The ghastly nights since her and Orion's rescue, and the bad weekend she had just put in, apparently showed on her face, Drew realized. Larry was about forty, a dedicated family man and a pretty decent guy to work for. But he wasn't normally eager to listen to tales of woe.

Drew saw down. "You haven't been told what really happened at Black Creek."

Larry leaned back in his chair. "I haven't?"

"The whole thing was my fault, and I'm sick of Orion's lies. The ranch wasn't on his schedule, Larry. I deliberately deviated from his flight schedule so I could get him on LeBeau land. The copter developed a problem with the fuel system, a clogged line. Orion told me not to land, to turn around and head back, but I made the decision to set down, anyway. The debris from the windstorm made the landing extremely hazardous. My point, Larry, is that Orion never would have been put into that kind of jeopardy if I hadn't taken him outside of his own schedule."

Larry's eyes had narrowed. "I see."

"I wanted you to know."

"You took an unnecessary risk."

"As it turned out, yes." Drew got up and went to stand at one of the windows in Larry's office. "I'm not ordinarily so impulsive."

"No, you're not. You must have had a good reason."

"I thought so, at the time. In retrospect, it's as stupid as everything else I did."

Larry stood up. "Don't be so hard on yourself, Drew."

She turned. "Is that it? I thought you'd be mad."

"What do you want me to do, notify the FAA? Or put you on suspension? Negligence is a valid cause for dismissal, but you weren't flying government property. And I'm not sure a little side trip could be labeled negligent, anyway. It wasn't your fault the chopper developed mechanical problems."

"I know, but..." Drew dropped her eyes. She didn't know what she wanted, not from Larry, not from anyone. She had never been unhappier in her life, and she had believed part of her mood was because of concealing guilt.

If that were the case, however, she would already be feeling better, and she wasn't.

"Well, I'll get out of your hair," she said quietly. "Thanks for listening."

"Drew, why did Orion tell everyone that going to the ranch was his idea?"

Her eyes flashed. "Because he's a jerk, that's why!"

"A jerk? He protected your professional reputation and he's a jerk?"

Her attitude sounded inane, coming from Larry. And, Lord help her, she couldn't explain. She forced a weak smile and started for the door. "I've got work to do. Thanks for hearing me out."

"No problem, Drew."

Nick sat at his desk and stared at the papers in front of him. The sales contracts blurred in the intensity of his own thoughts. The days at Black Creek wouldn't leave him alone, Drew LeBeau wouldn't leave him alone.

Memory was an insidious thing sometimes, he was beginning to believe. Throw in a massive load of guilt, like he was carrying around, and a man had a hell of a time concentrating on anything else.

He'd treated Drew badly. He'd handled the whole thing miserably. How could he have made love to her and then ignored her? She wasn't a tramp, a woman to bed and forget. Without rescue that morning, he would have explained his feelings to her, but that was small comfort now. He'd even been putting off a meeting with her brothers, because the thought of facing Judd and Simon was nerve-shattering, and his nerves were already dangerously frazzled.

Nick knew what was lurking in his system, along with so much guilt and regret his stomach felt as if it was in flames most of the time: He had to see Drew and attempt to make her understand. An apology was the only thing that would heal his battered conscience.

He told himself again and again that they were both adults, and that Drew had wanted no less than he had. At moments the concept relieved his anxiety, but the relief was always temporary. He'd behaved like a jerk, or worse, some sex-starved cretin, and no amount of rationalization would make it right.

Locating her home address hadn't been a problem. It was written in his own file on the LeBeau land purchase, for that matter, along with being listed in the Laramie telephone directory. He had scrawled it on a small card and put it in his wallet. Calling her wasn't an option—when and if he worked up the courage for the confrontation, he would talk to her face-to-face.

Drew tried valiantly to get on with her life. She went to work every morning, she came home every evening.

But she was refusing invitations and spending most of her free time alone. The knot of anger in her midsection wouldn't relent. The carefree part of her had seemingly been destroyed. She was no longer a woman who laughed easily and found pleasure in simple pastimes.

Nights were the worst. Her job kept her occupied during the day, but at night she remembered, and walked the floor of her house while drinking cups of cocoa or herbal tea.

On Friday evening, steeling herself for another empty weekend, Drew took a hot bath and got into her pajamas and robe. Some friends had called earlier, coaxing her to go out with them. But she wasn't yet ready for a night of dancing and other people's gaiety. Eventually, she prayed, the hatred in her system would abate. Remaining embittered for the rest of her life seemed an awful price to pay for a few days of recklessness.

When the front doorbell rang, she was in the kitchen, waiting for the water in the teakettle to boil. Frowning at the thought of unexpected company, she switched off the burner and wound through the house to the front door.

She opened it and then stood there frozen, doubting her own eyesight.

"Hello, Drew."

Her heart sped up to the point of bursting. The possibility of Nick Orion appearing on her front stoop had never entered her mind. Her thoughts tumbled over one another. His good looks registered, his jeans, blue shirt and black boots. His expression was guarded, wary, but also strangely hopeful. Her own reactions were both physical and emotional. Everything was mass confusion, spinning in a daze of pain and anger and awareness that the cause of her misery was within reach.

"You bastard," she said low and furiously. "Get off my property!" She gave the door a forceful push, intending to slam it in his despicable face.

Nick caught it just before it latched and he stood on one side of it with Drew on the other, each of them determined to control its direction. "I just need a few minutes of your time," he growled through the narrow opening.

"I don't give a damn what *you* need! Get away from this door!"

"Drew, please. I know you're mad..."

"You don't know anything about me!" she shouted.

"Yes, I do. And you have every right to be angry. But I have a right to explain."

There wasn't an explanation in the world that could excuse what he'd done, and she wouldn't forgive him even if he had wracked his brain and come up with something that sounded plausible. It would only be another lie, anyway.

"Go away! I'm warning you, I'll call the police!"

"Drew, listen to me, please. It wasn't easy coming here. Let me come in for five minutes. You can time them. I just want to talk to you for five minutes."

Maybe she wanted to hear his lies, Drew pondered around the over-fast beat of her heart. Maybe she wanted to look for that opportunity to pay him back. She would never find it, if he stayed on his side of town and she stayed on hers. They lived and worked and played in different circles, and Laramie was big enough to completely avoid someone forever, particularly if one were determined to do so.

Nick studied the situation. If she absolutely refused

to see him, there was little he could do about it. Standing on her front stoop and arguing through a crack in the door was just plain silly.

"All right, fine. I'll leave you alone." He let go of the door, and Drew's weight shut it at once. He started down the three steps to the sidewalk, but stopped and turned when he heard the door opening again.

"Five minutes," Drew said stonily.

His blood pressure went up a notch. He hadn't apologized to anyone for anything really important in a long time. Eating crow for Drew LeBeau was going to be tough.

But once done, he'd sleep better at night and get a lot more work accomplished during the day.

"Thanks."

Drew watched him take the three steps, then stood back so he could come in. She closed the door behind him. "Go on into the living room," she said coldly.

Having him in her own house was traumatic. She was so emotionally torn up, she could easily break down and do something moronic right now, like crying. And if she shed even one tear in Nick Orion's presence, she would never forgive herself.

Nick stood in the middle of the living room. Drew folded her arms across her chest and leaned against the wall near the arch to the foyer. "Five minutes," she reminded flatly.

She was standing there like a prosecuting attorney, all righteous and certain of her case. But she was wearing a pink robe and her face was shiny clean and pretty, and memory stirred his senses. He knew what the robe concealed. He knew how her body responded to his touch. She claimed he knew nothing about her, when the truth was that he knew too much.

He looked away and raked his hair with suddenly tingling fingers. It was disconcerting to realize that Drew's physical attraction was still present. Why should she bother him so much, when no other woman had for so many years?

Drew was enduring uncomfortable thoughts, also, memories she wished she could rip from her mind and destroy on the spot. It wasn't fair that the first man she had felt so much for had turned out be a snake.

"I guess what I came here for was an apology," Nick said in a low, tension-filled voice.

"An apology," Drew repeated evenly. She mustered up a smirk. "I already apologized, but if that's what you want, fine. I'm sorry for..."

"Not from you! From me."

His aghast expression was almost funny, although right at the moment there wasn't a laugh anywhere in Drew.

"Drew, I..." How did a man say he was sorry for making love to a cooperative woman? How did he explain feelings he didn't understand himself?

He tried again. "I know you're not the kind of woman who...What I mean is, what we did at the ranch..." He raked his hair again and paced a small circle. "Damn, this is hard!" He stopped abruptly. "Drew, I know I hurt you, and that's what I'm apologizing for. I don't go around hurting people, and it's been driving me nuts."

The words had spilled out of him, Drew saw, as though a dam had broken. But Orion's defense was a crock. If *he* didn't hurt people, who did?

"So," she said coolly. "What would you like me to say now? That I understand? I don't. That I've already forgotten? I haven't."

"No, of course not." Nick tugged at his ear. "I just wanted you to know that I regret the incident."

The incident. Well, of course that's all it was to him, an "incident." And now that he had apologized, he could pretend it had never happened.

Resentment broiled in her system, but, cruelly, so did memory. And while pretense might eradicate that night for Nick, she would never forget it. She could have loved this man…dammit, she *had* loved this man. And he had twisted it into something ugly.

But he would never know how deeply, how abidingly, her pain went. No one would ever know the degree of humiliation she was living with. She wasn't a one-night stand and never would be, even if that's how Nick Orion had treated her.

As far as returning the crushing blow went, what could she ever do to hurt him in kind? Men like him breezed through life—and through women—without a qualm. Actually, his apology was surprising.

Drew managed to maintain a stoic expression. Nick had obviously run out of steam and was looking at her with an oddly helpless gleam in his eyes. He'd said what he'd come to say, apparently, and was waiting for dismissal or…some-thing.

That one small note of uncertainty on his face aroused Drew's curiosity. Surely he wasn't thinking of something further between them! He couldn't possibly have the nerve to mention friendship, could he?

Her pulse beat quickened. She had seen his gaze traveling her robe several times. Not that the garment was at all suggestive. A long, bulky chenille bathrobe was hardly conducive to romance, certainly nothing she would have chosen to incite a man's interest.

But Orion *was* interested!

The thought nearly staggered Drew. In spite of his apology and discomfort over the whole affair, Orion was still interested! She couldn't believe it, but when she really let herself *see* Nick, without rancor, without resentment, the signs were clear.

He was as close to fidgeting as any man she'd ever seen, shifting his weight from foot to foot, fiddling with his shirt buttons, absolutely destroying his hair with nervous runs of his fingers.

But along with all of his obvious tension was an unmistakable aura, something felt, not seen. A woman knew when a man was seeing her *as* a woman, and that's what was bothering Nick Orion just as much, if not more, than his acute discomfort about his apology.

Something smug and satisfying warmed Drew's insides. She had found her weapon, a method of revenge, if she had the intestinal fortitude to go after it.

It would take some thought, she decided, but she would pave the way, just in case.

"Thank you for coming by," she told a startled Nick Orion. "What happened between us wasn't any more your fault than mine. I appreciate the apology."

Seven

Nick drove away from Drew's neighborhood with a deep frown of perplexity. She'd done some sort of about-face with him, and he couldn't unravel its meaning. Did her thanks for his apology indicate genuine forgiveness? If they ran into one another somewhere, for instance, would she say hello?

At least, now, he felt better about going ahead with the LeBeau land purchase. He would call Judd within the next few days and set up an appointment to iron out some final details on the transaction.

Wait a minute, he thought, with a sudden jolt. How come Drew hadn't been included in the other meetings he'd had with Simon and Judd? The family owned the property jointly, which meant she had as much say in its disposition as either of her brothers.

His initial contact had been with Judd. Along with Simon, a sister had been mentioned, but Nick had gotten the impression that the woman was leaving the matter in her brothers' hands.

Now he wondered. That detour Drew had forced on him obviously involved the ranch. Why else would she have taken him there?

But to what purpose? When she'd tried to explain, he'd cut her off. If he asked for an explanation now, he had the feeling she would cut *him* off.

There was only one thing to do, insist that Drew LeBeau attend any future meetings concerning Black Creek Ranch. He would inform Judd of that decision the next time they talked.

"No, Judd, absolutely not! You and Simon have handled it thus far, you can continue doing so without any help from me!"

"Drew, be reasonable. Orion said you have to be there."

"Why?"

"I thought you might know."

"Well, I don't. Call Orion back and tell him I'm not getting involved."

Judd was sitting in Drew's kitchen, looking disgusted and out of sorts. "When you get something in your head, you're as stubborn as Old Tillie."

"Old Tillie" was a mule the LeBeau family had once owned, and a more stubborn, ornery animal had never graced the face of the earth. Being likened to Tillie was hardly a compliment, but it wasn't the first time one of the LeBeaus had relied on the mule for a comparison. Every one of the LeBeaus had a stubborn streak a mile wide, Judd included.

Drew had to laugh. It was an old crack, and funny, a family joke.

"I just don't understand you," Judd said morosely, obviously not nearly as amused by his reference to Tillie as Drew was. "When you weren't included in the deal, you fought tooth and nail. Now, when everyone wants your input…"

Drew's smile faded. "Neither you or Simon want my input, Judd, so stop with the sad face."

"Orion wants you there, dammit! He as much as said, no Drew, no meeting!"

The sale of the LeBeau land was important to her brothers, Drew realized again. And maybe they were right. For certain, *she* hadn't been right.

At any rate, it didn't matter anymore. Her aversion for a place she had loved, was another very substantial reason for resenting Nick Orion.

She had been thinking about her flash of inspiration the evening he came to her house. Tempting Orion into an emotional trap might be exactly what he deserved, but it also smacked of deceit and treachery. Deliberately setting out to lure a man into falling hard, just so she could ultimately laugh in his face, was pretty strong stuff.

Besides, she had vowed, at the ranch, to never do anything again without looking at it from every conceivable angle. She had let emotion override common sense with that episode, and barreling into another situation without weighing the consequences was out of the question.

What if *she* was the one who got hurt? What if the feelings Orion had brought to life at the ranch returned? What if those feelings grew and expanded?

But that idea was too preposterous to consider for long. Like Nick Orion? *Love* Nick Orion? The mere thought of him turned her stomach. No, she wasn't apt to feel anything for the man but contempt.

Still, she didn't like being pushed into a meeting with him, especially when it was him doing the pushing. For some reason, Orion was manufacturing bullets and using Judd to shoot them. Why he should suddenly insist on her presence at a business meeting was a mystery, but maybe there was something to ponder in that aberration, too.

Whatever, Judd wasn't going to leave without a positive answer, Drew saw from the determined glint in his eyes. And maybe she just didn't give a damn anymore.

"All right, you win," she said wearily. "When is the meeting?"

Judd got to his feet. "Then you'll come?"

"Yes, I'll come. When and where, Judd?"

The meeting was to take place in Orion, Inc.'s main office. Drew arranged her schedule to leave work at three on the appointed day. The weather had turned unusually warm, and she was wearing off-white cotton slacks and a sleeveless blue blouse. She had recently visited her hairdresser for a trim, and her style was crisp and fresh-looking. Other than fancy clothes, her appearance was as good as it got, she believed, and then became annoyed that she would care.

She drove to the correct address, parked outside the building and went in, assuring herself repeatedly that she didn't give two hoots what Nick Orion thought about anything, let alone whether she looked good or not.

Inside, she saw five or six people at desks, which were separated by shoulder-high room dividers. A friendly receptionist greeted her. "Your brothers are already here, Drew. I'll show you to Nick's office."

Apparently "casual" was the company's motto, because everyone—other than the receptionist—was in jeans and boots.

George Hollister appeared in the corridor. "Drew, how are you?"

"Fine, thank you." She shook Hollister's hand, uncomfortably aware that he still believed Nick had brought her to the ranch, not the other way around. An urge to tell him what really happened was nearly intolerable.

"This way, Drew," the receptionist interjected, with a smile.

Guilt plagued Drew during the short walk to Nick's office. Judd and Simon should know the truth, too. She hated being treated like a heroine, when she had been the villain.

More than that, though, she hated the convolutions of her own mind every time she tried to figure out why Nick had lied about her role in the fiasco. None of the possibilities was at all flattering to her.

Nick was behind a massive desk, and he stood up when Drew entered the room. Judd and Simon stayed in their chairs, but gave her a nod and a thanks-for-following-through grin. She smiled faintly at her brothers and took the third chair at the front of Nick's desk.

"We were discussing right-of-ways, Drew," Nick volunteered.

"Go right ahead. Don't let me interrupt."

She looked as distant as the stars to Nick, but there was no denying something warm and vital in his own system, just because she was sitting across his desk.

The conversation ebbed and flowed around terms

Drew was only vaguely familiar with. Such as "title insurance" and "deeds of trust" and "mineral rights." She only half listened. Judd and Simon knew what they were doing, and her input would only consist of questions, if she offered any.

She simply did not care what happened to the ranch anymore, and while it seemed sad to Drew, she couldn't alter her attitude.

But she would never forget that it was Nick Orion who had stolen such a simple pleasure from her. How smug he looked, how superior, sitting behind that big desk.

For that matter, the three men in this room were so much alike it would be amazing, if it weren't so nauseating. All her life she had put up with male condescension, struggling to maintain control of her own preferences. Judd and Simon had gone so far as to attempt to choose her friends in high school. And they were still telling her what to do.

Not that she listened to them. She lived her life according to Drew LeBeau, not her overbearing brothers. But to think that she had fallen for a man with the same domineering traits was abominable.

What each one of the big, macho he-men in this room needed was a good strong dose of reality, and she would love to be the one to dole it out.

Drew sighed. Her brothers were really her sisters-in-law's problem, not hers, and if they didn't gripe, why should she? Orion, on the other hand, she thought with slightly narrowed eyes, was a whole different ball game.

Maybe her idea had some merit, after all. There was no way she could ever be attracted to Nick again. She saw through him now, as clearly as if he were constructed of glass. Tough on the outside, overly confident on the inside, too sure of himself, positive that God had created women solely for men's pleasure. And to order around.

Like this meeting, for instance. What possible reason could have occurred to him to force her presence here this afternoon? Was she adding anything to the conversation?

Nick slid a paper across the desk. "This will open an escrow with the title company. I'll need all three of your signatures."

Drew's eyes met his while Judd read the paper, and she found herself shaping a slow smile. Orion's reaction was astounding, a start of disbelief and, then, a relaxation of his entire body, a returned smile, very warm, very friendly.

Judd scribbled his signature and passed the paper to Simon, who also took a few moments to read it.

Drew studied her fingernails, which were short but neatly manicured. She glanced around Nick's office, deciding it was comfortable and efficiently arranged, then looked at him again. He was staring at her, as if he hadn't stopped staring since her smile.

Simon signed his name and slid the paper to Drew. "It's fine," he told her. Judd chimed in. "You don't have to bother reading it, Drew. It's only a formality to open escrow."

Judd and Simon had read it, but it wasn't important that *she* understood the paper's content. For a second Drew nearly rebelled. A picture of herself standing up and stating firmly that she wasn't signing anything concerning the ranch, not ever, flashed through her mind. It would rock these three arrogant men back on their heels. Without her signature, the deal would be a dead issue.

But none of them would take such obstinacy lying down, her brothers, especially. How Orion might react was merely a suspicion in Drew's mind, but Judd and Simon were as predictable as the seasons.

And she honestly wasn't up to the kind of warfare they were capable of declaring.

With the same pen Simon had used, Drew scrawled her name on the blank line below her brothers' signatures.

Nick reached for the paper. Drew saw his expression was satisfied, as he tucked the document into a rather flat file folder. Judd and Simon got to their feet, and Drew followed suit. Apparently the meeting was over.

The LeBeau men shook hands with Orion and filed out of the office. Drew was almost out the door when Nick said, "Wait a minute, Drew."

She turned with an arched eyebrow. "Yes?"

Her expression was daunting, a complex mixture of challenge and patronage, as though she knew something he didn't. He had absolutely no understanding of Drew LeBeau, Nick admitted uneasily. In spite of having made incredible love with her, her mind was a complete mystery. What was she thinking right now? What was behind that raised eyebrow and the slightly cynical cast in her striking green eyes?

She had said very little during the meeting, appearing more disinterested than anything else. Insisting on her presence had probably been a bit heavy-handed, and he should have let the LeBeaus handle their side of the transaction without interference.

"I know you were bored," he told her. "You don't have to attend any future meetings." He remembered the smile she had shown him. "Unless you want to, of course."

His eyes contained a strangely hopeful light. Instantly Drew recognized an opportunity to give him a taste of his own cruel medicine. Instead of telling him she would do almost anything to avoid seeing him again, however, she heard herself referring to the paper she had signed. "I suppose I was needed today."

Nick advanced a few steps. "Yes, but the document could have been brought to you. Drew, I feel like such a jerk with you. I guess I was hoping we could be friends."

The word had finally come out of his mouth, *friends.* She had always valued friendship, but the concept of friendly give and take was ludicrous for her and Nick. Did she want him dropping in, as her friends did? Would she ever ring him up on the spur of the moment and suggest taking in a movie, or going to a high-school basketball game?

Actually, she wasn't calling *anyone* on the spur of the moment these days. She felt splintered inside, raw, irreparably damaged.

And she did not want to be friends with the person who had caused so much pain. Was he really so dense that he didn't comprehend the enormity of what he'd done to her? Was a night in bed with a woman merely another night to him?

She was such a fool, and she hadn't known she could behave so stupidly.

"I suppose we could be friends," she said slowly, startling herself. *That* wasn't what she'd been thinking, not even close! She wasn't herself with Orion. She didn't speak her mind, at all!

"Do you ordinarily fly for other people outside of your regular job?"

"Pardon?"

"I was just wondering if you were interested in some extra work. On weekends, maybe."

She was dumbfounded. "You would trust me to fly your helicopter again? With you in it?"

Nick wondered where his brain had fled to. Trust Drew LeBeau at the controls? The image of him hanging on for dear life made him wince inwardly. The idea had come out of nowhere. It was just that he didn't want her walking out of here without something resolved between them. She bothered him. He thought about her too often. Maybe it was only sexual. No one could question the flawless sexuality the two of them had attained at the ranch.

There was no "maybe" about it. What he felt for Drew LeBeau was *completely* sexual. Didn't she feel it, too, that hum of electricity? That magnetic tug? The tension in the air that felt like an excruciatingly exciting promise?

Drew had never separated sex and romance before, and there wasn't a heart or a flower anywhere in sight. There hadn't been at the ranch, either, but she'd smelled roses all the same.

"I'm not looking for extra work," she said flatly. "But thanks for the offer."

Nick breathed a furtive sigh of relief, then tensed again when she started to leave. "Drew...uh...let's have dinner some evening."

She couldn't believed it. The man was asking for a date, and she honestly couldn't believe his gall. Drew leaned against the door frame and looked at him. He was begging for a sucker punch if anyone ever had.

What, in heaven's name, did he think was going to happen? A quiet little dinner for two and then another night of lust?

Revenge was well within reach and appearing more logical by the moment. Wouldn't she feel just a little bit better about the whole thing if she succeeded in denting his massive ego? Wouldn't she be striking a blow for every woman who had ever been emotionally destroyed by a man?

"All right," she heard herself agreeing. "Call me."

Nick was already thinking about his schedule for the rest of the week. Tomorrow night was relatively free. He had no specific appointments, at least.

"How about tomorrow?"

Drew hadn't expected something so soon. "Oh... well..."

"Maybe you already have plans."

Her positive nod was some sort of automatic defense mechanism, because she had no plans, whatsoever. But she was beginning to feel uncomfortable at the thought of "dating" Nick Orion. Her ambivalence was mad-dening. Relishing revenge in her own mind was a far cry from going through with it, she was discovering.

"I better be going," she mumbled. "Goodbye."

Nick followed her down the corridor and opened the building's front door for her. "I'll call," he promised, as she scooted past him.

It wasn't until she was in her car, that Drew faced the tremors in her system. It was an internal sensation, a disturbing weakness, the sort of feeling one had after a roller-coaster ride.

Orion was a roller-coaster ride, all right, and she had rocks in her head to even think about fooling around with him for revenge. The man didn't even *like* her, for pete's sake! He'd made that very clear before getting physically carried away in front of the fireplace. But he'd take her to bed again, probably in a heartbeat. Was that what she wanted? To be treated like a tramp again?

She despised him! Drew bit her lip. She did despise him, didn't she? Why was she trembling? Why was she remembering how incredible his naked body was, and how it had felt wrapped around hers?

Tears filled her eyes. She hadn't healed at all. She might *never* heal.

Angry that she should still be so torn up over a man who deserved nothing but scorn, Drew wiped her eyes and started the car. Somehow, she had to forget everything that had happened at the ranch.

Nick stood at his office window. Beyond the glass, the sun was starting to go down. An unusual yearning was keeping him restless. The day had been a total bust, a dozen tasks still awaited his attention, but he hadn't been able to concentrate since his meeting with the LeBeaus yesterday.

He hadn't felt so on edge in years. Building the business had been immensely satisfying. Sure, he'd worked hard and with few diversions. Yes, he'd more than likely developed the start of an ulcer. But success demanded a price, and he'd been willing to pay it.

Now...he just didn't know. Financial goals didn't seem so important. Nothing looked quite the same as it had, not his life-style, his work, his own attitude.

He never should have touched Drew LeBeau, and why had he? She wasn't so gorgeous as to elicit awe in any man that saw her, and God knew how upset he'd been with her feckless behavior. Literally, the woman had made him see red.

But he'd forgotten her faults, and his own aggravation, in a wild night of passion. Why? He'd never had a problem with his libido before that. Since, his moods had been weird, incomprehensible.

Impossible to ignore was that Drew was behind every other thought, constantly lurking in the shadows of his own mind. She had sidestepped a definite date, after agreeing to dinner together. Maybe he, himself, had provided her with an excuse with his reference to "previous plans," but he didn't behave normally around her.

He wanted to see her again. If the yearning in his belly was strictly sexual, so be it. She hadn't been exactly uncooperative that night, and there was a mystery in her smiles that raised his blood pressure.

Some of his people were back at their desks after a dinner break. Nick had planned to work late, too, but he wasn't any more productive this evening than he'd been all day.

Maybe Drew really did have plans and wasn't at home. But if she was...?

With a determined gleam in his eyes, Nick left the window, his office and finally the building. He got into his Wagoneer, started it and pointed it toward Drew's neighborhood.

Eight

It was a beautiful evening, warm and velvety, a rarity in Wyoming. Drew was sitting outside. Her house had a redwood patio, which contained an umbrella table, two chairs and a lounge. As pleasant as the evening was, Drew was full of sighs.

She knew that she had to start living again. Some of her friends were beginning to wonder about her refusals to participate in activities in which she had always taken an avid interest. She was wallowing, not in self-pity but in painful memories. They always concluded with one soulful question: How could she have been such a fool?

People didn't fall in love as quickly as she had, and especially not with a cold, crass individual such as Nick Orion. All he'd done was touch her, and she had totally lost all sense of reality. At moments her humiliation went so deep, she wanted to disappear.

Disappearing wouldn't be a simple matter, however. Her job was important, her family and friends were here, and she had her house to consider. She couldn't just walk away from responsibilities and family, not even to relieve her own misery.

But she couldn't go on the way she'd been doing, either. Avoiding friends had to stop. She would plan something for the upcoming weekend, call a few people, do a little cooking. Learn to laugh again. To chatter about nothing important, or to debate and discuss world affairs.

Life had been good before Nick Orion, only she hadn't realized just how good.

The windows on the back of the house were open, as was the kitchen door. Through the screens, Drew heard the pealing of her front doorbell. She wasn't expecting anyone, but now was as good a time as any to begin that change of heart she'd been facing as necessary and sensible.

Putting on a smile of welcome, she skipped through the house and opened the door.

The first thing Nick saw was Drew's dress. So far, he'd seen her in slacks, a blanket and...nothing. The pastel-print dress she was wearing made her look different, more feminine, softer.

The second thing he saw was the way her face was losing a shade of color, and how her smile was vanishing. He'd taken her by surprise.

"You're home," he said quietly.

She cleared her throat. "Obviously."

He tried to smile. "I didn't call like I promised, but I was wondering if you'd take a ride with me."

"A ride where?"

"Nowhere in particular."

"Nick...no." Her heart had started beating like a tom-tom. "I...can't."

His gaze drifted over the pretty dress. "You're going out?"

"Uh...no...yes...no!" Why was she stammering? She didn't owe Nick Orion anything. Her eyes bravely met his, but only briefly. Looking away again, she mumbled, "I'm tired."

"Hard day?"

He was trying to be nice, Drew realized with a sinking sensation. She didn't *want* him being nice.

And she didn't want to get in his car and go for a drive with him, either. Once burned by Nick Orion was quite enough, thank you very much!

As for that foolishness about seeking revenge, she was beyond playing games with the man. With *any* man, for that matter. It would be a cold day in hell before she succumbed to masculine appeal so easily again.

"Drew, maybe I can never really atone for what I did at the ranch, but I'm trying. Will you give me that?"

Embarrassment suddenly choked her, but right on its heels was anger, which she welcomed. "Maybe I don't care if you're trying."

"I don't believe you're that unforgiving."

Drew's eyes flashed. "And maybe I don't care *what* you believe! Were you forgiving at the ranch? I tried to explain why I wanted you out there, and you wouldn't listen. Did you forgive me? You barely spoke to me!"

Nick began cringing at the onset of Drew's outburst, and by the time she stopped for air, he wanted to sink into the ground. He'd gotten her all fired up, that was

certain, and there wasn't an unfair accusation in anything she'd said, either.

"I'm sorry," he said weakly. "That's all I can say,
Drew, I'm sorry. I had so much to do that day. You
have to admit your methods are a little unorthodox."

There was no denying his shock when he understood
how stuck they were, Drew recalled. Regardless, Orion
had been a stinker! And he had the nerve to talk about
her unforgiving nature? His tongue should fall out!

She opened her mouth to tell him so, but then he
grinned, and darned if he didn't look as if he was trying
to tease! "Let's be friends, Drew. We started out bad,
I know, but I think we've got a lot of potential."

Drew's stomach recoiled. He was referring to that
one mad night of lovemaking, and how dare he have
so much audacity? After totally ignoring her the next
day? After all but telling her straight out that she meant
nothing to him?

She had never really spoken her mind on the matter,
but if he stood at her door much longer, Drew knew
she was going to do just that. It wasn't that she wanted
to scream at Nick. She much preferred him leaving her
entirely alone, but it was becoming increasingly ap-
parent that he had different ideas.

Some harsh words were about to spill out, when a
car drove up and stopped behind Nick's vehicle at the
curb. Drew's gaze swept from Nick to Simon's wife,
Julie, as she got out and called a cheery, "Hi!"

Julie sauntered up the front sidewalk. "Hello, Nick.
How are you?"

Drew stared. She honestly hadn't known that her
brothers' wives were acquainted with Orion. Julie was
carrying a book, and after chatting briefly with Nick,

she held it up. "I brought over that novel I told you about."

"Thanks." Drew could see the curiosity in her sister-in-law's blue eyes, the questions. Clearly, running into Nick Orion on Drew's front stoop was a surprise.

Drew knew that she could keep Nick standing around indefinitely, but not Julie. "Come on in."

"Can't. I only stopped for a second." She passed the book to Drew. "I'm having a little get-together on Sunday, Drew. Mike and Cindy are driving up from Denver. We'd like to have you there."

Mike and Cindy were cousins, people Drew had always enjoyed seeing. "Thanks, I'd love to come," she said.

Julie smiled at Nick. "Why don't you come, too? It's nothing special, just food and conversation, but I know Simon would like having you there. Judd, too."

Nick glanced at Drew's less-than-inviting expression, the don't-you-dare-accept gleam in her eyes. "Thanks, Julie, I'd like to come."

"Dinner should be ready around two. I'll probably set up a buffet."

Drew sent Nick a murderous look. "Can I bring anything, Julie?"

"Sure, if you want to. How about a pan of those great brownies you make? The kids love your brownies."

"I'll make a double batch."

Julie grinned. "See you both on Sunday."

Her sister-in-law's grin was definitely intrigued, Drew saw with annoyance. A new element had been added to an ordinary family affair for Julie LeBeau, who wasn't at all above matchmaking even without such a golden opportunity.

This whole thing had to come to a screeching halt before it got out of hand, Drew thought. She didn't want Nick mingling with her family. Thus far, his association had been strictly business. One Sunday with the noisy LeBeaus could very well alter his status, and running into Nick at her own brothers' homes would be an aggravation she didn't need.

With a pleased-as-punch smile, Julie said "so long" and sauntered back to her car. Nick waved her off, as though they were old friends, and Drew stood there glaring.

"You're too damned nervy," she announced heatedly, as Julie drove off. "I don't want you mixing with my family, and you knew that when you accepted Julie's invitation."

"I like your family, and it has nothing to do with you."

"Of course you *like* Judd and Simon. Why wouldn't you? The three of you could have been triplets!"

Nick frowned. "What's that supposed to mean?"

"Figure it out for yourself!" On the verge of exploding, Drew stepped back to slam the door. Preferably in Nick Orion's smug face.

Nick reacted without thinking. Grabbing the door just before it latched, he stepped up onto the threshold and forced the door open again, pushing Drew back at the same time.

"Don't you dare force your way into my house!" she cried.

But he had, and he was standing with his broad back to the closed door and wearing an obstinate expression. "You're a hard woman, Drew. One mistake and you write people off."

She *wasn't* a "hard" woman, except with overbearing males, and Nick's assessment stung. But, then, had he done anything at all that hadn't hurt her in some way?

"If you've changed your mind about us being friends, say it straight out," he said harshly.

"How plain do you want it?"

His eyes narrowed. "Why the sexy smiles, in that case?"

"Sexy smiles! Don't flatter yourself!"

"I know a come-hither smile, when I see it!"

"Are you really so full of yourself that you interpret every smile from a woman as an invitation? Get real, Orion! Join the human race! Find out that most of us mortals have feelings, even if there's a few like you who walk around like damned zombies!"

"I'm no zombie, which I think you know very well."

"Because you're so smooth in bed? Making love doesn't make you a real person, Orion. The real challenge comes afterward."

"Maybe the real challenge is right now," he muttered, and moved quickly, hauling Drew up against him with the swoop of two strong arms. "I don't know any other way to get through to you," he growled, and brought his mouth down on hers with no regard for her indignant sputtering.

Nick's brashness was infuriating, but he was bigger, stronger, and a wrestling match would be ridiculous. She would endure his despicable kiss and embrace, and then he'd get a blast that would scorch his ears!

It didn't go quite according to plan, however. The kiss set off something in Drew's system, a buzzing and yearning that softened her spine and her lips. In mere seconds she was kissing him back, leaning into him, molding to the firm, masculine lines of his body.

Then she was up against the foyer wall, and Nick's kisses were falling on her throat, her forehead, her cheeks. Tears sprang to her eyes, tears of self-reproach and frustration. How much emotional abuse would Orion have to dish out before she didn't physically respond to his touch?

Nick's lips encountered a tear, and he raised his head to look at her face. He wasn't breathing easily, and neither was Drew. They ignited something in each other, a wild kind of passion he had no previous experience with. He didn't know what to make of it, and he could see from the devastation on her face, neither did Drew.

"Don't cry," he whispered, knowing she was as shaken as he was. "Something's happening with us."

"You're *making* it happen."

"No one could force what I'm feeling right now."

Her wet eyes looked into his. "I know exactly what you're feeling, and I won't play the fool twice. I'll never get involved with you again."

They were still squeezed together, his body caressing hers. "You want to," he whispered. "You're feeling the same things I am."

"Let go of me."

He didn't want to let go of her. He wanted to kiss her again and again, and feel her response, and take her to her own bedroom and make love until they were both exhausted. There was more here than ordinary desire, something that touched his soul.

But there was so much animosity in Drew, so much anger. He might entice her into bed again, but the anger would still be there.

Slowly he dropped his arms and gave her some space. "Will you talk to me?"

Self-disgust gave her voice a sullen tone. "What about?"

"About what happened at the ranch."

She laughed derisively—that, too, for herself. "What could we possibly have to say to each other about that sickening episode?"

"It wasn't sickening!"

Drew moved away from the wall and him. "We obviously remember it differently." She faced him from a safer distance. "You and I are not ever going to be friends. I should have made that very clear right away. I don't like you, Nick. You're cold and unfeeling, and this sort of thing scares me."

"Wanting me, without liking me," he said softly.

"That sums it up pretty well."

"Don't you wonder why we affect each other so strongly?"

Drew's eyes flashed. "I *wonder* where my brain is hiding! With your cavalier attitude toward sex, you probably could never understand, but I don't sleep around with just any man."

"Don't you think I know that? That's exactly my point, in fact. What made you respond to me that night?"

She swallowed. No way was she going to tell him about her ludicrous thoughts of love that night. "I wish I knew," she said coolly. "No, I take that back. I'm simply not interested. I made a mistake with you— several, to be precise—but I won't compound them with further involvement. And I would appreciate your staying away from my family."

"I have to see Judd and Simon."

"I'm talking about socially, which you well know!"

Nick rubbed his mouth thoughtfully. "Tell me why you brought me to the ranch that day."

"Why?"

"Because I want to know! Dammit, Drew, you're the most irritating woman I've ever known!"

"So sue me," she muttered.

Nick shook his head. She wasn't going to give an inch, and maybe he couldn't blame her. "I'd rather kiss you," he said softly.

Drew felt a flush rising. Her mouth was still warm from his other kisses, her body still tingling. Her weakness for Nick was some sort of horrible flaw she hadn't had to face before. Why him? Why, of all the men she'd known, past and present, was he the one to bring that flaw to the surface?

Wonder why he affected her so strongly? You bet she wondered! Hadn't she been driving herself crazy with that very question?

"Nick...please go," she pleaded, sounding much less in control than she liked.

He folded his arms and leaned against the wall. "You're a puzzle, Drew, and I've always been drawn to puzzles."

"You might not like the solution," she said sharply.

"And then, again, I might like it just fine. I intend finding out, you know."

"No matter how I feel about it?"

"Maybe I know how you feel, better than you do. Or better than you'll admit."

"Just when did I become so interesting?"

Nick thought for a moment. "You were interesting right away, but you were also so irritating I wanted to paddle your behind."

"Which was why you were so obnoxious? Well, it's a good thing you didn't try it!"

He grinned lazily. "And if I had?"

"I didn't grow up with Judd and Simon without learning how to defend myself."

Picturing Drew in combat with either one of her brothers raised a laugh from Nick. Judd and Simon LeBeau were both big guys, and Drew couldn't weigh more than one-ten soaking wet.

Oddly enough, Drew found herself wanting to laugh, too, but she stifled the urge. Laughing with Nick Orion would be almost as traitorous to herself as kissing him was!

Still, the atmosphere wasn't nearly as tense as it had been. Drew let out a small sigh. If Nick was determined to push himself into her life, there really wasn't a whole lot she could do about it. She certainly wouldn't get any help from her family, not without some very direct confessing, which she couldn't do for any reason.

"Are you really going to Julie's on Sunday?" she questioned warily.

Nick pushed away from the wall. "Sure am."

"Someplace along the way, I've gotten the impression that you don't waste time on such mundane activities."

It was the God's truth, or it had been. Drew's appraisal gave Nick a start, but he couldn't deny it. "Maybe it's time for a change," he allowed. "I'll be there, Drew. Count on it."

"It will be a madhouse," she warned. "Mike and Cindy have three kids, and with Judd's son and Simon's two daughters..."

He hadn't thought about the kids. A flicker of pain

darted across Nick's features. Katie would have been ten this year.

"I like kids," he said quietly, and walked to the door. "Sure you won't change your mind about a ride? It's a great evening, Drew."

"I'm sure," she said, wondering about that strange, fleeting expression she had caught on Nick's face. It had disappeared so quickly, there and gone, but it had denoted a part of Nick she had never seen before.

Then, there had to be a hundred aspects of Nick's hard personality she hadn't gotten near. One second of exposed vulnerability meant little.

She felt his gaze, the intensity of his dark blue eyes, and she lifted her chin. "Goodbye."

"Only for now, Drew."

"Maybe it's one day a time with you, Nick."

"Maybe it is, but that's not such a bad policy, is it?"

"I'm not going to get involved with you again," she repeated.

"The thing is, honey, I think we're *already* involved."

"Speak for yourself."

He looked at her, then smiled and nodded. "Fine. I'll speak for myself and you do your own speaking. I'll communicate anytime you say the word. How about right now?"

"No."

"That's what I thought. See you on Sunday."

Drew returned to the patio in a very unsettled mood. Nick upset her. It was perfectly obvious what he wanted from her, but did he really think she would fall into bed with him again? His opinion of her was the most insulting she had ever encountered.

Still, she had brought it on herself. Drew's expression became brooding. Nick's kisses this evening had been shattering. In spite of resentment and outrage toward the man, she reacted to him in a startling way. How could that be? How could her mind and body work in direct opposition? Maybe it was more a question of mind and emotions, although there again, had she become so weak-minded that she was led by emotion?

Painful to face was what might have been. Imagining herself in love that night at the ranch had been ridiculously premature, obviously, but the remnants of those strong feelings were still in her system. If Nick had felt the same, they would now be deeply and immutably tied to each other.

Maybe she was looking for that sort of relationship with a man, Drew had to admit, although the concept hadn't pestered her in the past. But she was thirty-one years old, and it would be sad if marriage and babies totally passed her by.

Thinking of babies caused a frown. She had made love without protection, and a little over two weeks had dwindled away. Her monthly visitor was due. Envisioning the worst—an unplanned pregnancy—created a riot of fearful emotions. She had been a fool in more ways than one that night.

What on earth would she do in such an untenable situation? It *would* be untenable for her. She couldn't even bear the thought of abortion, let alone consider it an option. And she could never go to Nick, never! Her brothers would be in an uproar, demanding marriage, probably confronting Nick, certainly nagging at her. All hell would break loose in the LeBeau family.

"Damn," she whispered. Pregnancy had crossed her mind before this, but not with such a vivid progression of thoughts. Maybe her life wasn't hers to plan anymore. Maybe fate was already in control and directing her future.

Leaving Laramie would probably be her only choice, as disturbing as the prospect was. She would not battle her brothers and public opinion and maybe Nick, too. Not that she could see him falling all over himself to do the honorable thing. But even if he offered, the thought of a forced marriage with a man like Orion made her shudder. He might have more than his share of sex appeal, but his sensitivity wouldn't cover the head of a pin.

Drew lifted forlorn, tear-misted eyes to the stars that were beginning to appear in the evening sky. She was going to pay for her reckless behavior with Nick Orion for a long, long time. Even if she wasn't pregnant— please, God!—she would never forget.

Nine

Drew arrived at Julie and Simon's house shortly after noon on Sunday. Everyone, except Nick, was already there, and the whole clan appeared from wherever they'd been to greet her. She kissed and hugged each of the six kids first, then the adults. The LeBeau family had always been pretty demonstrative, and even Judd and Simon, as big and gruff as they were, were usually receptive to a hug.

The kids ran outside to play, the men went to the living room, and the women headed for the kitchen. It would be a standard family get-together, Drew knew, which meant the women cooked and gossiped, the kids had a ball playing together, and the men drank beer and watched football or some other sport on TV. If Nick fit into that scenario, she would be eternally surprised.

Lois, who was Judd's wife, and Julie and Cindy returned to their interrupted tasks. Good smells drifted on the air, along with female chatter and laughter. Drew washed her hands and dived into the melee to help out wherever she could.

It wasn't long before Nick's name came up. "You had a close call at the ranch, I understand," Cindy said in a tongue-in-cheek tone. "Julie and Lois tell me that Nick Orion is quite a hunk."

Drew had expected something like that. Her adventure at the ranch was bound to come up for discussion, and Nick's good looks definitely added spice to the episode.

The thing was, the three women in the kitchen didn't have a hint as to how tightly Drew's "close call" was beginning to pinch. She could very well be pregnant. What if she said it right out? she pondered in response to her cousin's teasing inquisitiveness. *Hey, gang, guess what?*

Instead, she smiled. "The landing was difficult. It's lucky Orion and I weren't injured."

"Yes, but what else happened?"

"What else?" Drew put on a bland expression. "Whatever could you possibly mean, cousin dear? Are you asking if Nick Orion and I slept in the same bed, by any chance?"

"Good grief, no! Drew, you know I was only teasing! But a good-looking man and woman alone for three days and nights? There had to be at least a little flirting going on."

"Orion doesn't flirt," Drew said flatly.

"But he likes you, Drew," Julie interjected. "I could see it on his face the other evening."

"I doubt it," Drew remarked dryly.

"Then why was he there?" Julie asked stubbornly.

Drew shrugged. "I have no idea why Nick Orion does anything. Nor do I care to find out. Frankly, I wish he wasn't coming here today."

Before Julie could reply, Cindy chimed in again. "Was he ever married?"

Drew looked to her sisters-in-law to answer that question. In truth, she knew absolutely nothing of Nick's past, but maybe they did. Both women shook their heads and admitted complete ignorance on the subject.

"Well, I still say the man is interested in you, Drew," Julie insisted. "Whether he was ever married before he moved to Laramie has no bearing on the present, anyway."

Maybe it did and maybe it didn't, Drew was thinking. Orion was an enigma, no two ways about it, and a bad marriage might make a person wary of the opposite sex.

Actually, since the other evening, she had been teetering in several directions on the subject of Nick and her possible pregnancy. The thought of cutting every tie and leaving Laramie was so painful she had been considering alternatives, every one of which would have to involve Nick. There was no way her having a child wouldn't arouse her family into some sort of protective action. Her brothers might be overbearing, but they weren't stupid, and it would take them about three seconds to figure out who the father was.

The bottom line was, if there was a baby on the way and she stuck it out in Laramie, she would need Nick on her side. Not as a husband, God forbid, nor as a lover. Not even, in all sincerity, as a true friend. But if she and Nick, as the mother and father of their child, were united in adamant opposition to a loveless marriage, even Judd and Simon would have to back off.

The one aspect of that conjecture gnawing at Drew was Nick's statement about liking kids. Just how much say would he demand in the care of his child?

It was all speculation, of course. Until she knew for sure, she wouldn't relate any of her worries or suspicions to anyone. Especially Nick.

The day passed pleasantly enough. Other than a rather cool "hello" when Nick arrived, Drew didn't find it too difficult to avoid him. The food was great and everyone ate until they were stuffed. The family camaraderie was relaxing and enjoyable, and Drew had to admit that Nick fit in a lot better than she had anticipated.

She registered two events that left a rather perplexing impression. The first was when Simon offered a beer and Nick asked for a soft drink. The other three men were drinking beer, but Nick sipped soda and iced tea all afternoon.

The second event was when Nick got up and went outside. Through a window, Drew watched him talking and then playing catch with the kids. He stayed outside for an hour.

Throughout the afternoon, even while deliberately avoiding Nick, Drew was constantly aware of him. She knew when he laughed about something and she overheard his end of conversations covering everything from sports to politics. Judd and Simon were bending over backward to make him feel welcome, and Nick was returning the courtesy by enjoying himself.

By six, Drew was feeling a little lost. Nick had smiled at her a few times, but hadn't attempted any sort of approach. The man had a way with smiles, she realized uneasily, recalling the one in front of the fireplace that night at the ranch that had been her undoing.

Discomfiting, too, were the sly little looks she kept getting from her family—the women, in particular. Judd's glances were speculative, Simon's curious, but the women seemed to be thrilled with the situation and waiting for something to happen.

It wasn't going to happen today, whatever they hoped "it" would be, Drew finally decided. She began saying her goodbyes, making the rounds of everyone and politely but firmly combating their resistance to her going home so early in the evening.

"I've got a fresh pot of coffee brewing," Julie protested. "Stay a little longer. We'll play cards or something."

"Thanks, but I really have to leave. The day's been great." She kissed her sister-in-law's cheek. "Thanks loads."

Nearly everyone followed her to the front yard, even Nick, although he stayed on the porch. But he was watching her, Drew knew, which was what he'd done most of the afternoon.

She drove toward home slowly, feeling oddly empty. Maybe she should have attempted at least a *little* conversation with Nick. She was really so horribly mixed up about him, though. How could he have been so nice today, when he'd been such a jerk at the ranch? Outside playing catch with the kids, yet. Who could have guessed?

Well, he'd cinched friendship with her family, that was certain. None of them had ever seen his other side the way she had—the arrogant, brooding and downright rude man he'd been at the ranch. She'd known all along that she had stepped on his toes with that unscheduled detour, but until now she hadn't realized just how deeply his anger had gone.

As for making love the way they had, what man would refuse a willing woman clad only in a blanket?

She was rationalizing, Drew realized with a stiffening of her spine, making excuses for Nick's abominable behavior. How could she be so disloyal to herself? That blanket had been the only thing in the house to cover herself with. Orion had been the one to start things, not her.

That empty, lost feeling in her midsection was getting bigger. Something had been missing from her busy life for a long time, and for a few lovely hours at Black Creek she had believed she'd found it. She'd fallen hard, no question about it; her feelings had not been imagined or merely exaggerated by passion.

And she was getting very tired of crying over Nick Orion! Angrily, Drew brushed away the tears seeping from her eyes. Yes, she hated him, and, yes, she loved him! How could she be so wretchedly torn in such diverse directions?

Instead of continuing on home, Drew turned her car north and drove out of the city. *If I'm pregnant...If I'm pregnant...* The phrase repeated in her mind like some sort of ghostly litany. Other women had faced the same problem, her situation wasn't at all unique. Besides, her late cycle might merely be a false alarm.

She drove until the sun was almost down, then turned the car around and headed back to town. The long drive hadn't solved anything, but she was feeling a little calmer by the time she reached her own neighborhood.

It was dark and her street had few streetlights. There

were lighted windows in some of the houses she slowly drove past, but her own house and yard would be as dark as pitch. Drew sighed. She always left lights on when she went out at night. Tonight she would have to feel her way up the sidewalk and into the house.

Life had become too complicated, she thought ruefully as she pulled into her driveway and turned off the ignition. Nothing seemed simple anymore, and all because she had...

Her thoughts stopped with a yelp of fright as the passenger door of her car opened and a man climbed in. "You scared me half to death," she said angrily, as she recognized Nick.

"Sorry, but if I'd waited until you went in, you would have locked me out."

Her heart was still fluttering. "You might have given me some kind of warning." She narrowed her eyes, striving to see in the dark. "You were waiting for me," she accused.

"Obviously."

"What for?"

"So we could iron out a few things."

"Whether I agree or not, apparently. Don't you understand what 'no' means?"

"I'm very attracted to you, Drew. Does that mean anything at all to you?"

She felt herself wilting internally. The overall situation was an incredible burden, and it was undeniably getting her down. "Nick...I don't want to fight with you. Please just leave me alone."

"Today, while you were flitting around and making sure we were never close enough to each other to speak, I got to thinking about something. Drew..." He cleared his throat. "Uh...are you all right?"

"Am I what?"

"Uh…I'm not sure how to put this. But…is everything normal with you…you know…your female functions?"

Drew was stunned to momentary speechlessness. Not in a million years could she have predicted Nick worrying about her "female functions." It hadn't once occurred to her that he, too, might be suffering a few pangs over the risk they had taken.

Nick sensed that he'd struck a nerve, and he sucked in an anxious breath. "You don't know yet, do you?"

She was beyond lying, she realized, while a dull ache began building behind her eyes. "There's a chance. I'm a few days late."

Complete silence ensued, seemingly growing in density until it rhythmically resounded in her ears with the same pronounced beat of her heart. The darkness felt smothering. She couldn't see Nick's face, his eyes. "I'm going in," she said unsteadily, and reached for her door handle.

"No, wait!" Nick caught her by the arm. "Drew, we've got to talk about it."

She hesitated, not for him but for herself. If her fears came to pass, discussion was inevitable. Maybe it was best to get it out of the way right now.

The darkness was suddenly a friend. She could speak unemotionally. "All right," she allowed. "I've pretty much decided what I'll do if the worst happens."

"The worst? Is that how you're looking at it?"

She didn't want unnecessary detours from the main theme. "Don't start judging me," she said with some acerbity. "And don't try to imply that you're not as rocked by this as I am."

Nick drew a shaky breath. He was rocked, all right,

but there was a funny sort of elation in his system, too. The sensation wasn't defined or completely understood, but it was there all the same.

"Go on with what you were saying," he told her.

"If—and remember it's still very much in the iffy stage—if I am pregnant, I want only one thing from you. My brothers..."

"You've got it, Drew," Nick interjected quickly. "Don't worry about that."

Her mouth dropped open. "I've got what? You haven't even heard..."

"You're talking about getting married, aren't you? Giving the baby my name?"

The breath whooshed out of Drew in one enormously deflated exhalation. "I am not talking about getting married," she said in a strangled tone of voice. "That's the first thing Judd and Simon will think of, too, and that's the one thing that's not going to happen. That's where you come in. I want your promise not to side with them, if the you-know-what hits the fan. If you get all protective and noble and insist on getting personally involved, my brothers will..."

"Hold on," Nick put in harshly. "Correct me if I'm wrong, but isn't the father *already* personally involved? You didn't get pregnant all by yourself, lady!"

Drew's voice rose. "I might not be pregnant at all!"

"I know that, but you're sitting there telling me that if you are, it's none of my damned business! You're saying, 'Stay out of it, Orion. All I want from you is a little support with my brothers.' Well, listen to this, Drew, and listen well. If you and I made a baby that night, it's my baby as much as it's yours, and I'm not *going* to stay out of it! And you'd better believe I would side with Judd and Simon! I'm saying it right now, and I would say it to them. The second you find out you're pregnant, I'll be ready to get married!''

"Do you think I would marry a man I despise?"

"You don't despise me. You're ticked off and look-ing for a way to hurt me, the way I hurt you. Well, this is a hell of a way to do it. Who would you be hurting most, me, yourself or the baby? Raising a kid without his father, just to avenge your own sense of outrage, would be unspeakably selfish.''

She was on the verge of hysteria. How dare he speak to her so callously? "This discussion is over,'' she said hoarsely. "Get out of my car and out of my life. I should have known how you would react. Let me tell *you* something, mister. If I am pregnant, you'll be the last person on earth to find out about it. I'll handle it myself, without your macho interference, without my brothers' macho interference!" She started to cry and began fumbling for the door handle again. "I won't marry you, no matter what you or anyone else does or says about it. Stick that in your pipe and smoke it!''

"Drew…damn…" Nick slid across the seat. She had succeeded in getting the door open, but he caught hold of her before she could get out. Sobbing, she struggled against him, but he brought her up against his chest and held her there. "I'm sorry. God, I'm sorry about so many things. Hush, honey. Don't cry. I know you're all tense and worried. I know you're mad at me, but try and get over it. There's a lot more at stake here than anger about the past. If there's a baby… Just think about it…a baby…Drew…"

"Stop," she pleaded. Crying into Nick's shirt was demoralizing, and her morale was already in shambles. She felt him kiss the top of her head, and a new wave of tears filled her eyes. His warm solidity was wreaking

havoc on her already ragged system. He shouldn't feel
so good. His touch should raise revulsion. She'd vowed
to say nothing about the possibility of a baby, and the
words had come tumbling out. She was getting in
deeper and deeper with Nick, which was in direct opposition to her rational decisions.

But he felt so comforting, so soothing, as if he had
vanquished some of her burdens. Or, at least, diminished their potency.

It was all becoming fuzzy, the heartache, the anger,
the worry. Drew released a shuddering sigh, a hopeless,
helpless sound. Like it or not, want it or not, her and
Nick Orion's futures could very well be irrevocably
entwined.

"Drew...I had a daughter once."

He'd spoken so softly, Drew questioned her hearing.
And yet she knew exactly what he had said. A daughter...once. "Once" was such an innocent word, but
Drew instinctively sensed its ominous meaning in this
instance.

The bottom fell out of her stomach. "You don't have
to tell me anything about yourself," she whispered
tremulously.

"I want you to know. My wife and daughter were
killed in a car accident five years ago."

"Oh, no." The denial was a hoarse moan, a com-
passionate cry that came from her soul. "Nick...I'm
so sorry." She wanted to say more. "I'm sorry"
seemed so inadequate. The tragedy of close personal
loss had struck her only twice, with the deaths of her
parents. The LeBeau family had been fortunate, otherwise. Nick's loss was so enormous it was almost incomprehensible.

His fingers flexed in her hair, caressing her scalp. A

responsive shiver danced down Drew's spine. "If you're pregnant, the baby will be important to me," he said gently.

Drew had hoped she was through crying, but tears began flowing again. Her heart was aching, for Nick and his sad past, for herself, for the situation. Of course he would care about his baby, even if he had very little feeling for its mother. Admitting attraction to her, as he'd done, indicated nothing beyond a desire to take her to bed again.

Lord help her, she thought with sudden, dizzying clarity, she could do it, too. In her case, to be fair to herself, there was more than an almost overpowering physical attraction. But "more" was so out of the question with Nick.

She had to get out of this car and away from Nick's pull. She had to *think!* "I've got to go in," she mumbled.

Nick hesitated but finally let go of her. "Do one thing for me."

Even a simple concession might be a mistake, and how many more mistakes dare she make with Nick? "What is it?" she questioned uneasily.

"Go to a doctor right away. Like tomorrow. Maybe you shouldn't be flying, if you're pregnant."

"I really don't think that's a problem." Drew knew of several women pilots who hadn't had to stop flying until their third trimester of pregnancy.

"Drew, please. See a doctor and find out for sure. What about those home tests I've seen advertised?"

"I've heard pros and cons on their reliability. I've been planning to see my doctor, but..."

"Then you'll call me?"

It wasn't a matter of choice anymore, Drew thought

with a wash of weariness. She, herself, had taken the matter out of the "choice" category.

"I'll call," she said dully.

"Tomorrow?"

"Whenever I can get an appointment."

Even with a cloak of darkness blurring features and body lines, Drew looked very small. Nick drew in a long, almost choked breath. He was moved by the situation, damned moved. No one knew better than him how strong and gutsy Drew LeBeau really was, but he was sensing an unfamiliar fragility about her tonight.

"I'll walk you to the door," he told her.

Drew didn't even attempt a protest. As hurdles and problems went, Nick wanting to escort her through the dark to her own front door seemed a lot more considerate than pushy.

The walk was short and cautiously accomplished. Nick hung onto her arm. "You should leave a light on at night," he remarked.

"I usually do." Drew had her house key ready and immediately inserted it into the lock upon reaching the door. "Good night."

"I'll be waiting for your call."

Without Nick's confidence about losing his family, Drew knew she would have said something flippant in response, something like, "Don't hold your breath!"

But there wasn't a sassy urge anywhere in her, nothing impudent or impertinent or brash. He had shocked the brass out of her, apparently, completely eradicating her normal starch.

Or maybe that self-protective trait had been diminishing even before tonight. Maybe it had started thinning out this afternoon at Simon's house, when she'd watched Nick tossing a ball around with the kids.

Pushing the door open, Drew reached around the frame into the foyer and snapped on a light. Unbidden, her eyes rose to meet Nick's. She hadn't known what she would see, but it startled her to recognize hope, to pick out concern and a strange sort of longing.

He wanted this baby! He would willingly and gladly marry her to have it!

A rush of emotion nearly staggered Drew. "Good night," she said quickly, and went inside and closed the door. Then she stood there and shook like a leaf. Nick Orion was no longer unreachable. If she wanted him, she could have him.

Not with love. He hadn't offered love, or even hinted at that sort of bond. But his proposal of marriage wasn't only to do the honorable thing. He *wanted* his child!

Drew's hands dropped to her lower abdomen. She *was* pregnant, she was positive of it! Her heart began beating a mile a minute. A baby and Nick. Would he be a good husband? A good father?

Where would they live? Where did *he* live now? Would he accept her affection for her job? She would take a leave to have the baby, but then she would want to find a capable sitter and return to work. How did Nick feel about working mothers?

For that matter, how did Nick feel about *anything?*

Drew's shoulders slumped with a sudden dose of very cold reality: Would any man be a faithful and considerate husband to a woman he didn't love?

She was begging for heartache. How could she be so damned gullible? Ten minutes alone with Nick and she started getting fanciful notions again. Had she gone loony, or just contracted a case of terminal stupidity?

* * *

Nick lay awake for hours. For years he hadn't let himself dwell on Mary and Katie. Tonight they seemed almost real again, and he let the memories flow. The good times. The laughter they had shared. The love.

He'd never given a moment's time to the idea of remarrying. His business had flourished because of total dedication. He couldn't be considered a wealthy man yet, but he was well on his way. And what, besides a growing bank account, did he have?

Oh, yes, he thought, with a wry touch of his stomach. He had the start of an ulcer. It was burning right now, but not as badly as it sometimes did. Along with a vague discomfort, though, he felt excitement churning in his system. That's what was keeping him awake, the thought of a baby, a family of his own again. A son, a daughter, it didn't matter which.

And Drew, of course. He pulled in a long draught of air, slowly, thoughtfully. Drew confused him. Their physical attraction was unmistakable, but there was a lot more to a successful marriage than great sex.

Nick's eyes narrowed. Was that what he wanted with Drew, a truly successful marriage? A marriage in name only, for the baby's sake, was entirely possible. Even if they lived in the same house, he could go his way and she could go hers.

But that wouldn't quite do it for him, would it? If he was going to take the big step again, he wanted it all, the sharing, the closeness, the communication. Even the disagreements and arguments that ended in kisses and apologies.

He'd been a square peg for too long, Nick admitted with a dark frown. But what kind of chance did he and Drew have? Getting married because of the baby would be forcing a relationship, and anything forced usually didn't last for long.

Drew had said it right out: she despised him. He'd put up a good, logical argument, and he still believed what he'd told her. *You don't despise me. You're ticked off and looking for a way to hurt me the way I hurt you.*

But what if he never got past that wall of anger she wore like a banner? Anger was a destructive force, which he knew from personal experience. Unless Drew got rid of it, the concept of a successful marriage was no more substantial than a handful of dust.

His own anger, his resentment of her shenanigans with his flight schedule that day, seemed so flimsy now. It all had been so real then and seemed so unreal now. She had interrupted his life, intruded so blatantly that he hadn't been able to digest it.

Then, that night in front of the fireplace, he had let nature take its course, even while knowing, *knowing,* he shouldn't touch her. The first time might have been somewhat out of his control, but going to Drew's bed to make love again had been completely selfish. Guilt had made him so miserable afterward, he'd sneaked away like a thief in the night.

He'd sensed too much in her response, Nick remembered broodingly. She hadn't made love like a woman who took her pleasure wherever she could find it. She had made love to *him*. In spite of loads of antagonism for each other, she had felt something for *him*.

He'd rubbed her nose in it the next morning. In front of her brothers and the other men, his silent denial of anything important between them had been deadly.

That's what she was clinging to now, maybe deliberately, maybe without intent. Whatever, it was a seemingly insurmountable deterrent to a normal relationship.

It was, quite likely, one of the biggest problems he'd ever had to face.

Ten

Drew came out of the medical center in a daze. The test had been negative; she wasn't pregnant!

She found her car on instinct, then sat in it and stared blankly, seeing nothing. She'd been so sure. How could she have been so certain and so wrong?

She'd questioned the doctor. *I'm sorry you're disappointed, Drew, but the test results are conclusive. Have you been under some sort of unusual stress, lately? You're a healthy young woman, and an occasional interrupted cycle is well within the real of normalcy. But stress might cause it. At any rate, if nothing happens within two weeks, come back and see me.*

It was strange to face just how deeply disappointed she really was. She should have been thrilled, relieved, not disappointed.

Actually, in her present mood it would be easy to sink even lower, Drew realized unhappily. Depression had never been a problem for her, but things were looking awfully bleak right now.

Which was utterly ridiculous. When, exactly, had she switched from panic to joy over a pregnancy she certainly didn't need?

Nick had caused it, of course, Nick and his insistence on marriage if the test was positive.

Well, the test was negative, which effectively eliminated any such foolishness between her and Nick Orion.

Drew started the car with a heavy sigh. She had promised to call Nick with the test results and there was no getting out of it. She'd had some pretty frivolous thoughts about the two of them and marriage, embarrassing thoughts. Making love the way they had, with such intensity of emotion, for her at least, had left an indelible mark. From here on in, every man she met would be compared to Nick.

Not that Nick would come out best in most categories. But he would when it came to making love.

Count your blessings, she told herself irritably, while she drove toward home. Her reactions to Nick were the result of an abysmal lack of self-control, nothing more. Marrying the man would have been the worst possible thing she could ever have done. She was one fortunate woman, and she should be thanking her lucky stars.

It was nearly five when Drew went into her house and dropped her purse on the kitchen table. She eyed the wall phone just above the counter. Nick had called yesterday and given her a list of telephone numbers where he could be reached. *Try the main office first, then my home. Someone should know where to find me, but if not, try these other numbers.*

The list was lying on the counter just below the telephone. All she had to do was dial…and relate the doctor's verdict.

Instead, she sat at the kitchen table and covered her face with her hands. No baby. Even removing Nick from the picture, the test results were defeating. She hadn't realized how real the baby had become to her, how important. Her feelings in that regard had very little to do with Nick or anyone else. They had been between her and the speck of life she had visualized developing in her body.

And there was no speck of life. There was nothing but some crazy quirk of nature that had delayed her usual regularity.

Strangely, there were no tears. This went deeper than tears. This touched her soul in a completely unfamiliar way.

Putting off the call to Nick was adolescent. Deeply regretting involving him in this, at all, was an exercise in futility. Sighing forlornly, Drew finally got up and went over to the counter.

She plucked the handset from the wall receptacle and dialed quickly. Nick's receptionist put her through to his extension immediately.

"Drew?"

"Hello. I…" Words failed her. She swallowed and began again. "The test was…negative."

He didn't say anything. Drew clutched the phone to her ear and waited until she couldn't bear the silence any longer. "Nick?"

"I'm here. There's no chance of error?"

"None. The doctor was adamant." Her eyes widened at the muttered, almost unintelligible curse she heard through the phone. She had been right, she realized. Nick had wanted the baby. "I won't keep you," she said then, not speaking very steadily.

"Don't hang up. Are you all right?"

"Yes, I'm all right." It was a lie. She wasn't a bit "all right," actually feeling lightheaded from the enormous void in her system. "Goodbye, Nick." Drew put the phone down.

At his desk, Nick pulled the phone away from his ear and stared at the dead instrument. Then he dropped it on its cradle, got to his feet and strode out of his office. On his way past Molly, the company's receptionist, he mumbled something about going for the day, leaving her with a questioning expression.

The thought of dinner turned Drew's stomach. She swallowed two aspirin tablets with a drink of water, and decided on a hot bath. In the bathroom, she turned on the tub's spigots and began undressing, letting her clothes fall into a heap on the floor. Carelessly, she threw a handful of bath salts into the water, and the scent of heated lilac rose with the steam.

She stepped into the tub and sat down. The water swirled around her, and she laid her head back and closed her eyes. Nick had wanted the baby, *she* had wanted the baby. Neither had said so. Maybe he hadn't admitted it to himself, any more than she had.

Her thoughts went to the ranch. The final papers to transfer the LeBeau land over to Nick were being drawn up. She could think of the sale dispassionately now. It was strange how much she had changed since meeting Nick. What had been of dire concern to her before had little meaning now. She would never know exactly what Nick did with the Black Creek Ranch, because she would never return to see it.

But she felt a longing for the days when she could have freely gone to the ranch and absorbed its almost magical serenity.

The tub was full, and Drew sat up to turn off the water. Then she lay back again and let the hot water saturate her senses.

Maybe knowing a man like Nick was a good lesson for a woman. Could she look at the experience from that perspective? Wouldn't she be a little more cautious around men now?

Drew made a disgusted face. She'd never been *in*-cautious around men. Only one time in her entire life had she behaved so recklessly, and yes, it had been a harsh lesson.

It hurt to remember that she'd actually been considering a shotgun wedding. She was such a sucker for Nick Orion, a totally different person than she was with anyone else. He fired her emotions in a completely unique fashion. Everything in her became very intense with Nick, but one would think that recognition of her affliction would diminish its potency.

Apparently that wasn't the case.

Well, he was off the hook. She was, too, of course. Only, she couldn't drum up much enthusiasm for her barren state. Maybe she *was* demented in some odd way.

Drew desultorily reached for the bar of soap. She cocked her head at the ringing of her front doorbell. It was precisely the dinner hour, which ordinarily precluded drop-in visitors.

The doorbell rang again, a much longer note. Frowning, Drew stood up and grabbed a towel. Whoever was leaning on the bell was getting impatient. Her old chenille robe was hanging on a hook on the door, and she dropped the towel and yanked on the robe, tying the sash as she hurried to the front door.

"Hold your horses," she muttered, as the bell intruded one more time.

She barely had the door open when Nick whipped past her. "Well, don't be bashful. Come on in," she said with pointed sarcasm.

He whirled. "Tell me what the doctor said."

"I already told you." Drew closed the door. "The test was negative. End of subject."

"Are you satisfied with that diagnosis?"

"What does satisfaction have to do with it? Either you're pregnant or you're not. It's not a case of 'maybe she is or maybe she isn't,' Nick." Drew closed the lapels of her robe a little tighter when she realized that Nick's gaze was directed to her chest. "I don't think there's anything more to be said on the matter. You can walk out of here with a clear conscience. You offered to make me an honest woman, and what more could anyone ask?"

Nick's eyes narrowed. "Would you have gone through with it?"

"Would you?"

"Stop it, Drew! Just once, talk to me without trying to start an argument, okay? That chip on your shoulder is beginning to wear a little thin."

"You're no better! You're *worse,* in fact. Who wore the 'chip' at the ranch? You were so mean, I hated you!"

"Yeah, you sure acted like you hated me."

"That's really low, Orion." Drew headed toward the living room. "Go away. Who invited you here, anyway?"

Nick followed her. "Get dressed and go to dinner with me."

She turned to face him. "Damn, you've got a nerve! What makes you think I would want to have dinner with you?"

Their gazes locked. Drew's color rose, and she cleared her throat and looked away. She could shroud herself in any kind of self-protective emotion she chose, but Nick still affected her. "There's no reason for you to be here," she said weakly.

"Maybe there is. I don't think either one of us has really faced it, but something got started between you and me at the ranch and it hasn't gone away."

"That's silly," she scoffed, with all the bravado she could muster. "The whole thing meant nothing! Not this much!" She snapped her fingers.

"Oh, really? Then why were you so bent out of shape the next morning?"

"I was...surprised. Yes, that was it. I was merely surprised. Once I thought about it..."

Nick took two quick strides and stopped directly in front of of her. "You were bent, Drew, royally ticked. You're *still* ticked." He lifted a hand to her arm and let his fingertips travel a cord of chenille up to her shoulder. "I want you," he said huskily.

"I...don't want you," she whispered.

"I was happy about the baby," he said softly. "Happy about you." His fingers drifted to her hair, touching it here and there. "I haven't been happy like that in a long time. That signifies something, Drew."

"No...I mean...not for me." She'd been standing there in a trance, and only instinct made her duck her head and back away from him. "Don't do this to me,

Nick, please. I don't want what you do. I can't sleep around and pretend it means nothing."

"But that's exactly what you just told me that night did mean to you, nothing." He advanced again, stalking her as she retreated.

"Right. You're right. I'm not making sense, I know, but... Dammit, Nick, stop following me!"

"Then stand still!"

"So you can lull me into something?"

His hand curled around the back of her head. "Is that what I'm doing, 'lulling' you?"

"You want me to go to bed with you," she accused heatedly.

"You've got that right." He brought his face down and spoke with his lips an inch from hers. "I don't know what it is, but I can't stay away from you. I've tried. I've reminded myself what a pain in the neck you can be. I've told myself how sassy you are, and that a woman with your mouth could drive a man nuts.

"But that only made me think of your mouth, and how it feels under mine. And *that* made me think of how your body feels under mine. You see...one thing leads to another." His lips touched hers. "Kiss me. Let me kiss you."

Everything was getting all wavy and distorted. Her limbs were weak, her legs barely holding her upright. "I'm such a fool," she whispered brokenly, wondering why her strength would traitorously desert her in such a crisis.

"Maybe we're both fools. Maybe every man and woman who need each other are fools. It's a risk, honey. Giving yourself, exposing yourself." His lips brushed hers again, first in one direction, then the other.

His teasing kisses were creating a tumult of emotions

in both of them. Drew sucked in air. Nick was persuading her, coaxing her into making love. Why did he have so much power over her senses? Why hadn't she ever felt this melting weakness for any other man?

Her lips parted for the inevitable kiss, the one she wanted as much as he did. With a swift intake of air, Nick settled his mouth on hers. His arms moved and brought her closer, fitting her body to his.

A bolt of lightning couldn't have caused any more impact than Nick's full embrace. His hard thighs held hers, his chest flattened her breasts, and the red-hot evidence of how aroused he was burned between them.

His tongue plundered her mouth, hungrily, almost greedily. His hands began to roam over her back and hips. "Drew...oh, baby..." It was a gasp between kisses, a hoarse, ragged cry of desire.

She couldn't let this happen. Not again. Drew pushed on his chest for a moment, then doubted he'd even noticed. It had been a faint effort, she knew, but how could she resist him and her own self, too? He was honest about what he wanted, at least, and she hadn't been.

As though from a great distance, she felt her robe slipping from her shoulders. Not by itself. Nick had loosened the sash and was pushing the garment away from her heated skin. "No," she moaned, tearing her mouth from his. "Nick...no."

"Sweetheart...Drew..." His voice was as rusty as an old hinge. He held her, with robe askew and her shoulders, throat and the tops of breasts exposed to his gaze. "You're so beautiful."

"That's only...sex talking," she mumbled.

"Is that so terrible? What's wrong with what we have?" He tried to kiss the curve of her throat, and felt her wriggling to avoid his mouth. The robe gave a little more, baring one lush nipple. It was firm and peaked, Nick saw, fully aroused, as he was. "Drew...whatever you want...name it," he bargained thickly, and dipped his head to lick the sensitive crest.

Her mind spun to a dizzying plateau of intense pleasure. His tongue was sinful, tasting her, wetting her, thrilling her. She was fighting against nature itself and losing the battle. She wanted Nick in the most elemental way, naked and hot and exactly as he'd been that day at the ranch. What came before and afterward was fading again, eluding distinction. That was the key to his power, she realized. He made her forget everything else but the immediate present.

Her head went back and she shut her eyes. Her emotions were being whipped into a froth of yearning. His mouth became bolder, his hands, too. She sensed, without seeing, when he unzipped his jeans.

And then he moved her to the wall and completed the task of opening her robe. Her breath stopped in her throat when he lifted her and positioned her and finally entered her, and she allowed it all, needing him so much she was incapable of protest.

"Open your eyes. Look at me," he commanded hoarsely. "Let me see what you're feeling."

Her eyelashes fluttered upward, and she looked into the blue fire of his eyes. Her position was hardly graceful. One foot was off the floor, her leg held up by his hand. They were joined. He was deep inside her body, and it felt so incredible she couldn't speak.

He executed a slow slide, an outward-and-in-again movement, and the thrills in her body compounded. She finally managed a feeble, unnatural voice. "Are you going to withdraw...like you did before?" It was weakly stated sarcasm, an attempt to point out that another risk was exceedingly foolhardy.

"You make me crazy," he groaned raggedly. "How do you do that?" He was moving at a slow, steady pace now, watching her face, supporting her weight, keeping them both upright and relatively balanced through sheer strength. "I've never met anyone like you before."

"That goes double for me," she whispered thickly. Making love with a man she shouldn't be within ten miles of, in her own living room, yet, was pure idiocy. But if he stopped right now and left her, she would be in agony. When had she become so sensual? So attuned to sex and its almost unbelievable pleasures?

She began moving with him, squeezing responsively, and felt his trembling reaction. His mouth sought hers, and the kiss between them was hot and wet and demanding. Love entered her mind and she mentally slapped it away. This wasn't love, this was lust in its purest form. She had to remember that and stop twisting her weakness for Nick into something romantic. She had to accept what they had and forget about the rest. Either that or get out of Laramie.

Tears filled her eyes. Maybe the drama was only in her own mind, she thought sadly, but it was real enough for her.

The melancholy moment receded, but the tears remained. She was climbing the pinnacle; Nick was, too. He was moving faster, clutching her bottom. They were both winded, gasping for air.

The robe had completely disappeared somewhere along the way. She was naked, Nick was *almost* naked. Her grasp on any sort of reality had vanished with the robe, and she no longer cared, not about anything but what Nick was doing to her.

Then, just like that, he stopped everything. Drew's eyes jerked open. There was perspiration on his forehead and his eyes were glazed. "Your room," he breathed heavily. "We need a bed."

She was beyond objecting to anything he might suggest, and when he picked her up, maintaining their awkward positions, and began walking, she buried her face in his shoulder and clung to his neck.

He found her bedroom on his own, and when he was standing next to the bed, he finally separated their bodies. Dazed and dizzy, Drew found herself placed on her own bed. She stared while he tore off his clothes, unable to shift her gaze from what he was exposing.

He had a magnificent body, which no doubt had a lot to do with her fascination. Nick was firm and tight in all the right places. His arms and shoulders were well muscled, his chest was broad and deep and covered by a triangular patch of back hair. Narrow hips, long legs and feet. He had to be the most beautiful man in the entire world.

And she was totally gone on him.

She wanted to flop on her stomach and wail, to just let go and bawl her heart out.

She didn't get the chance to do anything. Nick slid down beside her and took her in his arms. His mouth unerringly covered hers, and the flames ignited again so quickly, she nearly passed out.

He began touching her, rubbing her skin, caressing her from shoulders to knees. She did the same to him, moving her hands over his body in a dreamlike exploration. His textures were mesmerizing, hair-roughened skin, velvety heat, everything blatantly male and deliciously satisfying.

He kissed her breasts, her stomach, the very essence of her femaleness. It was as if he were laying claim to her body, Drew realized vaguely, pronouncing it his.

Right at the moment, it was. She would regret this, she knew, but she couldn't get off the bed to save her soul. He looked at her and touched her intimately, he kissed her lips again and again. She wondered at his lack of haste. He'd been so impetuous before and now acted as if they had all the time in the world.

He looked into her eyes. "Tell me this isn't special," he whispered.

Something sank within her. "I can't do that."

"I didn't think so. Why do you fight me so hard?"

"I think you know why."

His lips brushed hers. "We're going to have to talk about it someday, you know. You're carrying around an awful lot of anger."

"Maybe." His hand curved into the nook between her legs, and she licked her lips as her pulse took off again.

"Tell me what you're thinking."

The tip of her tongue circled her lips again. "I'm thinking that you've won again. That you've made me want you again."

"That's not so bad, is it?"

"Right now it's not bad, at all."

"And tomorrow?"

She turned her head and looked away. "If I think about tomorrow, I might not want you."

His lips moved over her cheek. "Impossible," he whispered. "I'm beginning to think we might always want each other. What do you make of that?"

Her head slowly turned back, until she was looking into his eyes. "What do *you* make of it?"

"Don't sound so suspicious."

"Can you answer me?"

His gaze probed hers. "If you want complete honesty, I'm pretty confused about you and me. How about you?"

"Confused, too," she whispered, dropping her eyes so he couldn't read her real thoughts. For a few seconds there, a deluge of hope had struck her. She didn't want him to see hope in her eyes, not over him.

"We're good in bed."

"Yes," she agreed huskily, unable to deny it.

He hesitated a moment. "I have protection with me. Do you want me to use it?"

Her heart skipped a beat. Why would he ask such a question? Did he *want* to get her pregnant? Wasn't one scare enough for him? "I think it would be wise, yes," she whispered unevenly.

He began touching her again, unhurriedly, a slow dance of incitement. It wasn't necessary. If Drew had had the strength to push him away, she would already have done so. She wouldn't be lying naked with him, giving him everything he asked for.

But the touching was exquisite, both hers and his, and there was a part of her that wished it could go on forever. In this, they were close, and they weren't in anything else.

The pressure of such uninhibited foreplay was rising, however. She stroked him boldly and watched his eyes narrow and his breathing change rhythm. Almost roughly he spread her legs farther apart. He changed positions and dipped his head, startling her into a silent "Oh."

His tongue was sinful, she decided breathlessly, but in this, like everything else he did, she was helplessly caught in his spell. Almost instantly on the edge, she writhed and moaned. "Nick…"

He heard her cry, and reached down to his jeans. She watched with dark, silent eyes while he took care of protection. Then he moved on top of her and thrust into her waiting heat.

There would be no stopping this time, no interruptions for anything. They both knew that, and they stared into each other's eyes while they moved and rocked together. He watched her desire mount, her excitement, her torment, and felt his own. Her fingernails scored his back, and he whispered, "My little wildcat," and thrust faster and deeper.

They reached the top together, as they had before, as he'd known they would again.

It took long minutes of complete immobility to cool down, to catch their breaths.

Nick finally raised his head from the pillow beside hers. "Can I stay the night?"

"You want more?" she questioned in amazement.

"Don't you?"

She was utterly replete, physically sated, and she had neighbors to consider. "No, Nick."

"How about dinner? Have you eaten?"

It was all returning, who she was, who he was, and every minute of their unstable interaction, causing panic in her stomach and massive quantities of remorse. "Yes, I've eaten," she lied.

He was studying her face. "You want me to leave, don't you?"

"I didn't want you here in the first place."

He rubbed his thumb across her lips. "You speak your mind so well about some things."

"I didn't say anything you didn't already know. Please let me get up."

"You're not over it. You'll make love with me, but you won't forgive me."

"I wouldn't be making love with you, either, if you would stay away from me."

His eyes took on a brooding cast. "How should I take that?"

"Nick, I'm not talking in riddles. Don't look for hidden meanings."

His body was satisfied, his mind was not. Given a choice, he would stay and talk until morning. There were convolutions to their relationship that needed discussion, exploration.

But Drew had turned off on him. It was in the very air, that she wanted him out of her house as quickly as he could get up and dressed. She wasn't happy about being coaxed into bed again, and she wasn't going to participate tonight in any sort of heart-to-heart.

Sighing, Nick moved away from her. She was up and gone like a flash, and he wondered if she would even reappear again to say goodbye before he wandered off.

Eleven

Drew slept badly that night, similar to what she'd already been enduring with one notable exception: She believed that she fully deserved sleeplessness now. What was that remark she'd made about not playing the fool twice?

Where Nick was concerned, she would be a fool all of her life, she suspected. What cruel fate had destined her to fall for a man who had locked love out of his life? That's what had happened, Drew felt. Nick's method of dealing with grief had been to overload his mind with work. The effort had seemingly been successful, to the point of leaving very little room for anything else.

Oh, he'd be back. When he needed a woman again he would ring her doorbell, and fool that she was, she would probably fall into his arms.

Her life plan did not include a long-term affair.

Short-term, either, for that matter. But that's what she was involved in with Nick, right up to her eyeballs. If it got around and reached her brothers' ears, there would be hell to pay. Judd and Simon were saturated with their parents' old-fashioned brand of morality. She was, too, but even a strict moral upbringing hadn't stopped her with Nick.

Drew got up and showered, and discovered definite evidence that she no longer needed to worry about pregnancy. Her heart thudded dully. Hope hadn't died because she had tested negative, she realized sadly.

It was all so futile. She didn't like her situation in the slightest, but did she have the strength of will to tell Nick "no" the next time he came around? He was using her. He couldn't even say "I love you," in the throes of passion.

In front of the bathroom mirror, Drew stared into her own eyes. She looked no different. The scars, the worry, the pain were all on the inside. Nick's "honorable" proposal of marriage seemed in the distant past, far, far away. How would she, an ordinary woman, deal with such an extraordinary relationship?

It *was* extraordinary, wasn't it? Or was the unvarnished truth closer to the fact that she had led a remarkably bland life, as far as romantic escapades went? Didn't some of her friends change bed partners every so often?

It was just wrong for her, Drew thought with a heavy sigh. Sex without love was wrong for her.

So...what was she going to do about Nick? Did he even like her as a person? Their communication began and ended in the bedroom, which wasn't entirely his fault. There were some things she couldn't say to him, even when he asked point blank. Did she like him? Not love, but like? Was she over the hurt he had inflicted at the ranch that morning? The disdain and arrogance he'd shown her before that?

It was all still there, harassing her system, she had to admit. She'd forgotten nothing, forgiven nothing. And yet she had made love with him again. True, she understood him a little better now. The loss of a spouse and child would harden anyone.

If she was to believe him, he was confused about the two of them, stating that he didn't know why he couldn't stay away from her. His attitude wasn't the least bit comforting, as the only reason that made any sense was extremely unflattering to her: she was easy pickings.

Her morale was at an all-time low, Drew knew. If Nick was happy this morning, then damn him for being an insensitive clod!

Finally, ready for work, Drew went to the kitchen for a cup of instant coffee and a piece of toast. She had just put the teakettle on when the telephone rang.

"Good morning," Nick said.

His low, sexy voice did crazy things to her nervous system, but she spoke calmly. "Good morning."

"Everything okay?"

"Why wouldn't it be?"

"Don't answer a question *with* a question. Are you all right this morning?"

Drew hesitated, then decided that any more beating around the bush with Nick would just get her in deeper. "No, I'm not."

"What's wrong?"

"You...me...everything. Nick, I want you to stay away from me."

"That's not what you wanted last night."

"It's what I want this morning."

"Are you sure about that?"

"Will you listen to me for once? I'm not going to keep on making mistakes with you. You want a different kind of woman than I am, someone who can smile when you show up and smile again when you leave. That's not me."

"What do you want from me, Drew?"

"I think I just told you. Leave me alone. I don't know how to say it any plainer."

"I'm talking about, what would you want from *any* man?"

"You can't give it to me, Nick."

"Try me."

"I think not." The teakettle was steaming. "I've got to go. Please do as I asked. Don't come to my house again, and don't call. Goodbye."

Her hand was shaking, Drew noticed as she put down the phone. She wasn't over Nick, not by a long shot. She might *never* be over Nick, but one usually paid a price for complete folly.

She could only hope he would do as she had requested, leave her strictly alone.

Nick leaned back in his chair and lifted his boots to the edge of his desk. His gaze narrowed on the ceiling and stayed there, although he couldn't have told anyone what he was looking at. It was a blind stare, an absentminded activity that let him think.

Last night had been incredible, and leaving Drew alone was out of the question. But maybe he'd better give her a little breathing room. Relationships were give-and-take, he at least remembered that, and maybe he'd done a little too much taking with Drew.

She had verbally accepted his apologies, but she hadn't forgiven him in her heart. Some wounds went too deep to heal overnight. Over a few weeks, either. He really hadn't intended to administer a lethal blow at the ranch, but Drew had taken his withdrawal as one.

Nick rubbed his jaw thoughtfully. Drew was a complex woman. His one major experience with the opposite sex had been with Mary, who had been sweetly uncomplicated. The two women were as far apart in personality as two people could be. Mary had been softly scented rose petals and serene water. Drew was spinning, exploding fireworks and a high, stormy tide.

But it was Drew's emotional volatility that kept him keyed up. She was the most exciting woman he'd ever made love with, bar none. Their inauspicious beginning, those first frustrating days at the ranch, had set a bad tone for their relationship. If they had gotten to know each other without so much initial anger, things would be different now.

Then, again, if they hadn't been in a forced situation, he might have met Drew and never even seen her, as he did with the other women who passed through his life these days. For five years now, for that matter, women as females just hadn't been important. Drew was, and why he would be so attracted to such sass and brass was hard to figure out.

Their relationship jumped levels constantly. It was up, it was down, it was sideways. Last night, for an hour or so, it had felt just about perfect. Now, this morning, Drew had done another reversal.

Basically, at its very foundation, the relationship was flawed, maybe irreparably. It was probably his fault, although Drew had started the whole thing by hauling him out to Black Creek in the first place.

Nick frowned. What, precisely, did he want from Drew? Where, exactly, did he want the two of them to end up?

He would have married her if she'd been pregnant with his baby, but was a strong liaison—marriage, even—still lurking in the back of his mind?

She would refuse any such proposal, he suspected. What they had together was chemistry, and beyond that they hardly knew each other. They should be going out on ordinary dates, eating together, talking, learning each other's likes and dislikes. How could he convince her to do that?

Nick forced himself to get to work, but at ten he left the building and drove to a florist shop. He wrote a card and picked out a colorful arrangement of flowers for a late-day delivery.

It was a start, he figured. Most women liked flowers.

Drew's schedule for the day included two flights to Roundtree Mountain to deliver dozens of flats of tiny pine seedlings. The area had suffered a devastating forest fire the year before. Some burn areas were left alone to reseed themselves naturally. Others, like the Roundtree burn, because of certain soil conditions and weather patterns, were reforested by Forest Service employees and volunteers interested in the preservation of the environment.

Drew tried very hard to force her personal problems to the back of her mind and concentrate on her job. Today, though, the glory of flying wasn't enough to eradicate the dissension in her soul. Her thoughts progressed through the events at Black Creek and up to the present, again and again. She asked herself questions and searched for answers.

The awful truth was, she was putty in Nick's hands. He could probably talk her into anything if he tried hard enough. Telling him to leave her alone had been wasted energy. If he felt like leaving her alone, he would. If he wanted to see her again, he would do that, too.

The day wore on. Wearing dark-lensed aviator-style glasses against the glare of the forever blue sky and bright sun, Drew piloted two trips between Laramie and Roundtree Mountain. During the last leg of the second shuttle, she sighed over a possible solution to her dilemma: leave Laramie.

How many times in the past few weeks had leaving everything behind and starting over somewhere else occurred to her? The idea still didn't thrill her, but Nick was firmly entrenched in Laramie. It might be a drastic way of avoiding someone, and she didn't like the idea of running away from a problem, but remaining at Nick's beck and call was going to cause her a lot more misery than she deserved.

After she landed and secured the copter, Drew headed for Larry's office. She peered through his door. "Oh, good, you're still here."

"Just getting ready to go home. How'd it go today?"

Drew moved into the room. "Everything went well. Larry, I've been thinking of something."

"Yes?"

With some nervousness, Drew tugged at her left ear. "I've been thinking about…a transfer."

He grinned. "You're kidding."

"Well, nothing's certain. I mean, it's only a thought at this point, but if I did decide to leave Laramie, would a transfer be a problem?"

Larry shook his head. "It's no problem, Drew, *if* there's someplace to transfer to. You know the situation. Only a few Forest Service installations maintain air transportation."

"Yes, I know. What about Montana?"

"Possibly. Colorado's another possibility. But I sure haven't heard of any openings, have you?"

"No. I guess I was hoping you might have picked up some information."

"I'd hate to lose you, Drew, but if you'd like, I could do a little checking."

"Thanks, I'd appreciate it. Please don't say anything to anyone about this, okay? It's just an idea, and I wouldn't want it to get around until I've made up my mind."

"Sure thing."

"Good night, Larry."

Drew walked to her car with a pensive expression. Leaving Laramie might solve her problem with Nick, but how would she feel living somewhere else, away from everything and everyone she'd grown up with?

It needed a lot more thought, Drew decided as she tossed her purse onto the front seat and maneuvered herself behind the wheel. She realized during the drive home, however, that she did have an out if Nick pressed too hard. An ace in the hole. Whether she ever used it or not, that ace gave her a small sense of security.

Drew wasn't in the house five minutes when the doorbell rang. Frowning, she peeked through the blinds on the living-room window, and then relaxed because the young man on the stoop wasn't Nick.

But he was carrying a long florist's box, and a van

at the curb bore a sign: *Connie's Floral Shop. Flowers for Every Occasion.*

Her friends didn't send flowers. They could be from only one person.

Somehow, Nick Orion sending flowers just didn't compute. For a few seconds Drew stood there and tried to add up apples and oranges, then, sighing rather helplessly, she went to the door. "I have a delivery for Drew LeBeau," the young man said.

"I'm Drew." She accepted the box. "Thank you."

"You're welcome. Have a good evening."

"You, too." She brought the box to the kitchen and set it on the table, not at all eager to open it. Everything Nick did felt suspect to her. Obviously, he'd ordered the flowers after their conversation this morning. Was this sort of thing his next ploy?

She finally lifted the top of the box. A large bouquet of red carnations, daisies, bachelor buttons and baby's breath lay within a nest of palm fronds. It was a pretty bouquet, and there was a card.

Drew gingerly picked up the card and read it.

Drew,
If there was a way to go back and do everything over again, we would start at square one. See me. Talk to me.

Nick

The poignant message wasn't what she had expected. There was no flippancy, no hint of the overwhelming confidence she associated with Nick. Drew's throat was suddenly full. Picking up the flowers, she brought them to her face and inhaled their fresh, clean smell. *We would start at square one.* Was that possible for her and Nick? A new beginning?

Reflectively, Drew found a vase for the bouquet. While she arranged the flowers, the ranch came to mind. Turning against the place because of what happened there had probably been childish. She hadn't overreacted to Nick's coldness that heartbreaking morning, but maybe she hadn't handled the situation very well after that.

She was instinctively a fighter. Her hackles rose easily, she knew. Hurt feelings or pride made her resentful and stubborn. Automatically, she lashed out at the cause. It was second nature to defend herself. If she hadn't adopted that self-protective trait very young, her brothers would have ruled every facet of her life. She thought of her attitude as "independence." Judd and Simon called it "muleheadedness."

It was probably a combination of the two.

Over a week later, Drew was extremely puzzled. Flowers had been delivered twice more, each time with a card, but Nick hadn't called or appeared on her doorstep. She wasn't sure what a woman did in such a strange situation. Should she call him and thank him for the flowers? Maybe she should put a note in the mail, she pondered, but what would she write? *Thanks for the flowers, but please don't send any more.*

She really didn't know what to think about the man, and she went from work to home to a few social engagements with a gnawing perplexity.

The weekend was approaching again, and the ranch, along with Nick's unfathomable antics, had been bothering Drew almost constantly. The final sale papers were nearing completion, she had learned from Judd, which meant that the LeBeau land would soon pass into Nick's hands.

She had to see it one more time, she finally admitted. As it was now. Before Nick did whatever it was he did to property to prepare it for sale to the public.

By Friday afternoon of that week, Drew had made up her mind to drive out to Black Creek on Saturday morning. She would stay in the ranch house Saturday night and return to Laramie on Sunday. It would be her final visit to the old place, she decided, the end of an era. Turning it over to Nick without a private "farewell" seemed terribly disloyal to her parents' memory.

Drew was walking from the helipad to the administration building when Larry came rushing out. "Drew! Have you heard?"

"Heard what?"

"No, I didn't think you had. There's a fire in Black Creek Canyon, only a few miles from the Hoskins ranch."

Drew felt herself go pale. "Is it bad?"

"Bad enough. Fire fighters are already on their way to the area."

"You'll need me to help fly in supplies."

"Too chancy, Drew. We can't risk the copters in that narrow canyon. Supplies are on their way in trucks, approaching the blaze from the Hoskins place."

"I've got to call Judd." Drew started backing away. Judd and Simon had to be told. Nick, too, probably, although she would leave that chore to her brothers. A forest fire could be a disaster for every landowner in the Black Creek area. "It rained up there a few weeks back," she reminded Larry.

"Good thing, or the fire would be moving a lot faster

than it is. We're making the Hoskins ranch a fire base. I'll be heading that way shortly.''

Drew was several steps past Larry, anxious to get to a phone. "Is there anything I can do? I was planning to drive up to the ranch in the morning.''

"I don't think so, Drew. Maybe I'll see you up there.''

"You're sure you won't need the copters? I don't want to be gone if there's a chance I'll be needed.''

"Right now I'm sure. With enough manpower and a little luck, we'll keep the fire confined to the canyon.''

Drew nodded. "All right, fine. I'm going to run and let my brothers know.''

Larry went in the opposite direction, while Drew sprinted into the building. A little out of breath and with her heart beating overly fast, she sat at a desk and punched out Judd's telephone number. Petey answered. "This is Aunt Drew, Petey. Is your dad home?''

"He's outside.''

"Go get him, honey. Tell him it's important. I'll hold on.''

It seemed an eternity before Judd came on the line. "Drew? Something wrong? Petey said…''

"There's a fire in Black Creek Canyon, Judd. Men and supplies are on their way. I just found out about it.''

"Hell! How bad is it?''

"Apparently it's still only in the canyon. Larry told me the fire base will be set up at the Hoskins place.''

"Well, I better get up there. Does Simon know?''

"I called you first.''

"I'll call him, in that case. I better let Orion know,

too. Damnation! We sure didn't need this! Are you flying in supplies or anything?''

"Larry says not. The canyon's too risky. But I am driving up tomorrow…''

"Like hell you are! You stay put, Drew. If Larry doesn't need you, then stay in Laramie!''

Drew rolled her eyes. "Judd, please don't start giving me orders. Neither of us needs a squabble right now.''

"Meaning you'll do what you want. Drew, there isn't a reason in the world for you to get involved. Stay in town.''

"I was planning to go to the ranch in the morning before I ever heard about the fire, which, I might point out, is miles away from the house.''

"Forest fires are unpredictable. Anything could happen.''

"Judd, please. I'm not a child.'' She heard a very long-suffering, put-upon sigh from her brother.

"You could try the patience of Job,'' Judd muttered. "Well, I better get off the line and make those calls. Simon and I will be at the Hoskins place if you need us.''

"Fine. Maybe I'll see you up there.''

After Drew hung up the phone, she shook her head. Judd would never change. No matter what she did, he tried to channel her plans to fit his concept of acceptable behavior for his sister. Simon was nearly as bad.

She had placed Nick in that same overly macho category, but doubts were beginning to pile up. In all honesty, placing Nick in *any* category was getting harder to do. What did he think flowers every few days was going to accomplish? His cards continued to surprise her with their scrawled messages of needing to get to know each other. Of starting over, of doing things differently this time.

Beneath it all, Drew wondered what his true goal consisted of. Did he hope to soften her up with a bombardment of flower deliveries and then move in for the final kill?

It was a melodramatic supposition, Drew realized, but Nick confused her. Apparently, he was heeding her request to not call or drop by. But the flowers seemed like evidence of some kind of game to Drew, and she couldn't predict Nick's next move.

She kind of figured it would come out of nowhere, though. Whatever Nick did next, she had a strong hunch she would be caught off guard.

During the drive home, Drew decided not to wait until morning to go to the ranch. Her car was reliable, and driving after dark didn't bother her in the least. She knew the roads between Laramie and the Black Creek area like the back of her hand, and if she stayed in town, she probably wouldn't get a whole lot of sleep anyway.

When she reached her house, she went in and threw a few clothes and personal items into her duffel bag. Then she raided the refrigerator and pantry and filled a large sack and an ice chest with groceries. A pair of binoculars were tucked into the duffel bag, too, because she was positive the fire would be visible from the house. The entire packing procedure didn't take more than fifteen minutes. She carried everything out to her car, made sure the house was locked and then drove away.

Twelve

Drew arrived at the ranch house just before midnight. She had stopped twice, once for gas, a second time for a hamburger at a roadside diner. She was relieved to discover that Nick's influence was no worse up here than it was in town, a realization that struck her the moment she arrived.

The lights in the house weren't working, which didn't surprise her. Judd or Simon had probably turned off the generator the morning they had found her and Nick. Using a flashlight, Drew carried her duffel bag in and brought it to her bedroom.

The beam of the flashlight fell on the bed, which had been completely stripped of bedding. "Darn," she mumbled, putting down the duffel bag. Someone other than Judd or Simon—they never touched her bed—had obviously been up here since the day of rescue, and what had they done with the bedding?

She was about to start a search of the closets when a distant red glow through the window caught her eye. Bedding forgotten, she hurried through the house to the back porch. The fire was miles off, just as she had told Judd, but nestled among the coal black mountains as it was, it looked eerie and yes, dangerous. A dense, pink-tinged cloud of smoke hovered in the night sky above it. "Thank God there's no wind," Drew whispered.

The mountain air was chilly, and she shivered and went back into the house. She was exhausted, ready for bed, and she suspected she would sleep very well tonight.

The sheets, blankets and pillows had been stacked in a closet, she finally discovered, and she took them out and brought them to her bedroom. Placing the flashlight on the bedstead, with the beam adjusted at a helpful angle, she hurriedly made up the bed. She would start the electricity and water in the morning; tonight she was too tired to tackle that eccentric old engine.

Changing into the warm flannel pajamas she'd brought along took only a few minutes, and then she crawled into bed, switched off the flashlight and yawned sleepily. Her eyes closed at once, but jerked open after only a few seconds. A car was coming up the mountain road leading to the house!

She bounded out of bed, grabbed the flashlight and ran barefoot on the cold floor to a living-room window. She'd never been afraid up here, not of animals or intruders. The place was so far off the beaten path, no one had ever just wandered in that she knew of.

But someone was wandering in tonight, and the late hour made the intrusion just a little suspect. Squinting through the window, Drew switched off the flashlight.

Then it occurred to her that Judd and Simon might have decided to spend the night here, which was logical enough to reassure her somewhat overfast heartbeat.

But it wasn't Judd's or Simon's vehicle that pulled into the clearing; it was Nick's.

What was *he* doing up here? He didn't own the place yet!

Nick climbed out and looked at the dark, silent house. Drew's car was in plain sight, parked no more than three feet ahead of his front bumper. He reached into the backseat and dragged out an overnight case. He'd brought some food along, too, but he'd bring that in later.

He started for the house, carrying the overnight case and a flashlight.

Drew watched him coming with a taut, resentful expression. She clicked on her flashlight just as he came in the door, hitting him squarely in the face with the beam. "What are you doing up here?"

Nick ducked the direct beam, and shone his own light on Drew, grinning slightly when he saw the sensible pajamas she was wearing. His expression sobered at once, though. "More to the point, what are *you* doing here? I couldn't believe it, when Judd said you were ignoring the fire and coming up here in the morning. I went by your house, and figured out you'd decided to leave sooner than planned. Was that why you left tonight, so someone couldn't have the opportunity to talk some sense into you?"

"You've got some nerve! In the first place, it's none of your business where I go and when, and in the second, you couldn't talk me out of anything!" The baldfaced lie just popped out. Who knew better than she how influencing Nick could be?

"I thought you were smarter than this, Drew. Did you take a look at that fire?"

"It's miles away."

"And with a little wind, it could be in this area by morning."

"The wind rarely blows from that direction."

"You're an obstinate, bullheaded woman, determined to be right even when you're wrong."

"I picked up the habit from my brothers. Tell me you didn't drive all this way just to badger me." She was shivering. From the chill in the air and the cold floor against the soles of her feet, to be sure, but Nick had a lot to do with her discomfort, too. He was carrying a leather overnighter, which seemed like incontrovertible proof of his intentions, and she didn't want to share the house with him.

"I didn't come to badger you," Nick growled. "But I'm beginning to think you need a keeper."

"A keeper! Good Lord, you certainly didn't come up here to *protect* me, I hope! I suppose Judd put you up to this. What did he do, call and complain about his disobedient sister?"

"He didn't complain. Look, I'm tired. Let's continue this argument in the morning, okay?" Nick turned and then shone his flashlight on a wall. "What do you think of the paneling?"

"The what?" Drew frowned at the circle of light illuminating the unfamiliar texture of the living-room wall. "That's pine! Who put it up?"

"I had a carpenter come up here for a few days."

"*Before* you even owned the place?"

"Judd gave me permission. I've been up here several times in the past few weeks."

"You're the one who moved my bedding!"

"Do you object to clean bedding?"

"You had it laundered?" Nick poking through the house before it transferred ownership irritated Drew. The paneling on the living-room walls irritated her even more. Until the final papers were signed, this was still LeBeau property. Why hadn't Judd said something about Nick already taking over when she told him she was driving up for the weekend?

"I'm going back to bed," she said disgustedly.

"Good idea. We can talk in the morning. Or argue, which you seem to prefer over normal conversation." Nick started away, but instead of heading for the bedroom area, he went to the kitchen.

Drew followed, shining her light on Nick's broad back. He set the overnighter down and proceeded to the back door. "What are you doing now?" she questioned peevishly.

"I'm going to start the generator."

"You?"

"Yes, Drew, me."

"I'd better help. That old engine..."

"Has been completely overhauled. Go back to bed, Drew. There'll be power and water in a few minutes."

Astonishment kept Drew standing there while Nick vanished through the back door. He really *had* taken over. It wasn't more than three minutes when she heard the faint rumbling of the diesel engine. Tears sprang to her eyes. This was already Nick's house, Nick's ranch. Even that infuriating old engine was his.

She stumbled down the hall and into her bedroom, closing the door behind her. Her feet were freezing, her teeth chattering, and she quickly hopped into bed and snuggled under the blankets. From this room she couldn't hear the diesel motor, but she heard Nick when he came into the house. She lay still and listened to his boot steps, placing him in the kitchen for a while, then going through the house to the front door, leaving, coming back in to return to the kitchen.

Having him in the house changed everything. Why was he here, if not to chastise her for another reckless impulse? Not that the fire was that much of a threat. Yes, if a strong wind came up, anything was possible. But she'd helped out with enough forest fires to know that only a few ran wild. The woods were not tinder-dry, due to that heavy rainfall some weeks back. Nick hadn't had to rush up here to save her from anything, but he *had* rushed, and she had to question his motive. Especially when his only contact for over a week had been in the form of flower deliveries.

Turning to her side, Drew stared at the window with its distant rosy glow. She would leave first thing in the morning. Spending the weekend with Nick, if that was his plan, would totally destroy her last vestige of good sense.

Nick stretched out in his own bed with a big yawn. This was it, showdown time. Drew might try to flounce off in the morning, but there was no way her car was going to start. It might have been dirty pool to disable her car, but they were going to clear the air if he had to tie her down.

The conversation with Judd clicked through his mind.

"Nick, there's a fire in Black Creek Canyon. Near the Hoskins Ranch."

"How far is that from LeBeau land?"

"As the crow flies? Oh, I don't know. Probably a

good day's hike. Maybe two, depending on the weather.''

Nick *cocked an eyebrow. "Within hiking distance? That's interesting. Drew didn't mention that when we were stranded at the ranch.''*

"Well, she knows about it, same as me. Speaking of Drew, she's heading up to the ranch in the morning. For no damned reason, either. I told her to stay in Laramie. She flies supplies and men during some fires, you know, but Black Creek Canyon's a deep, narrow crevice, too dangerous to use the copters. Anyway, I don't like her going up there with that fire so close.''

"But she's going anyway.''

"She does what she wants, always has. Anyway, Simon and I will be at the Hoskins place. We're leaving in a few minutes. I just thought you should know about the fire.''

"I appreciate it.'' Nick *cleared his throat. "Judd, there's something you should know. Drew and I have been...seeing each other.''*

"No kidding? Hey, that's great, Nick. She never said a word. You know, she might listen to you. Maybe you should tell her to stay away from the Black Creek area. She'll be home tonight.''

"I was thinking about going to the Hoskins ranch, too.''

"Well, sure, but you could talk to Drew tonight and drive up in the morning.''

Judd's recommendation had made sense, and Nick had gone to Drew's house, only to find it locked and vacant. He'd known instantly what she had done. Actually, he'd been thinking of using his copter to get to the Hoskins ranch, but with Drew on the road somewhere between Laramie and Black Creek, he'd discarded that notion, dashed home for a few things and set out in his Wagoneer.

During the long drive, he'd come to a few conclusions. First of all, he cared what happened to Drew. Cared so much, in fact, it was time to stop kidding himself. What he felt for Drew was different than the feelings he'd had for Mary, but love didn't have only one definition.

Secondly, the anger between him and Drew had to be put to rest. This was the perfect opportunity to thrash it out. They would be alone at the ranch, ironically, exactly where it had all begun, and he couldn't have planned a better setting. No interruptions, not even a telephone.

Lying in bed and getting drowsy, Nick's system basked in the utter stillness. He'd come to love this old house, and he was fixing it up for his own personal retreat. The bond had sprouted during that first stressful stay here. After rescue, while diving back into the relentless routines of operating a demanding business, he'd remembered the peace of drinking hot tea in the middle of a rainy night.

He'd brought up a slew of men, a mechanic to overhaul the generator motor, a carpenter to install the paneling and to take measurements for some other renovations, men to clear the immediate area of debris. Drew would see what he'd started in the morning, although it might not mean much to her. The fire had drawn her up here, of course. Despite Judd's opinion that she was here for no good reason, she was undoubtedly too curious about the fire to stay away.

Nick thought of her in bed just down the hall and his body reacted predictably. If he wasn't so tired...

No, as great as sex was between them, what they

needed more was conversation. And she wasn't going to elude it this time.

Drew awoke slowly, stretched languidly and then checked her watch. Sunshine was pouring through the window; it was almost nine-thirty.

She lay there and remembered, with a noticeably faster heartbeat, that Nick was in the house.

But all was quiet. Not a sound penetrated the walls or closed door of her bedroom.

Her gaze moved around the room. Someone had torn away huge strips of the old wallpaper. Drew frowned, recalling the pine paneling in the living room. Nick was wasting no time in assuming ownership, obviously, but why was he spending money on the house?

Throwing back the covers, Drew got up and padded silently to the door. Through a small crack, she peered up and down the hall. The door to Nick's bedroom was closed. It seemed unlikely that he was still in bed, but if he was, maybe she could slip away without a confrontation.

Gathering up some things, she tiptoed to the bathroom and very quietly closed the door. Then she saw the piece of paper taped to the mirror. Leaning across the sink, she read Nick's increasingly familiar handwriting.

Drew,
Went over to the Hoskins place to check on the fire. Be back around noon. Hope you slept well.
Nick

"Jerk," she muttered, and tore the note loose to crumple it into a wad and toss it into the trash basket.

She had been planning on a quick wash, but with her reason for stealth gone, she might as well have her usual morning shower. Almost angrily, she began to shed her pajamas.

Nick riled her as no one else ever had. He'd followed her up here, of course. If he'd come solely because of the fire, he would have gone directly to the Hoskins place, as Judd and Simon had.

Thank goodness he hadn't made any fast moves last night. Whatever was in his mind was planned for today, and wouldn't he be ticked when he returned and she was gone? What an ego the man had, thinking she would just hang around and wait for him.

Drew stepped into the shower stall and lifted her face to the warm spray. She was really very tired of this whole thing with Nick. She didn't like male-female game playing in the least, she realized. Coyness was impossible for her. She might evade a subject, but she didn't know how to bat her eyes and sweet-talk a man into a *different* topic.

Maybe the worst aspect of their relationship was her dishonesty with Nick. Not out-and-out lying, but when had she ever really opened up and said exactly what she was thinking with him? That annoying habit had sprung up at their first discussion, when she'd held back all sorts of negative opinions about his rudeness, his impatience, his irascibility.

Thinking back to that awful morning when he'd literally turned his back on her, the old Drew LeBeau would have marched across the room and confronted him head-on.

Wouldn't she?

In front of her brothers and those other men?

Drew sighed. She had done the only thing possible,

pretended not to notice. Pretended her heart wasn't breaking. Pretended the night before had meant no more to her than it had to him.

It still hurt, damn him. And it hurt that she had so little self-control with him.

Well, he wasn't going to get another crack at her, not today he wasn't.

Turning off the shower, Drew brushed her wet hair back without drying it. She dressed quickly, bypassing cosmetics. Then she went to her bedroom, made up the bed and put the things she'd used back into her duffel bag, noticing the binoculars in the process.

Before she left she wanted a look at the fire, she decided, and took the binoculars to the back porch. The smoke was higher in the sky than it had been last night, rising into a thinning plume. With the binoculars trained on the area, Drew searched for flames.

She lowered the glasses with intense relief. The fire was being controlled, definitely slowing down. She could leave now.

Walking into the kitchen, she realized that the food she'd brought with her had been put away. The sack had been folded and laid on the counter, and the ice chest was empty.

She yanked open the refrigerator door and saw an impressive array. She hadn't brought those steaks, or that cheese spread, or that orange juice, or that…

Marching to her bedroom, she slung her purse over her shoulder, picked up the duffel bag and toted it through the house and out to her car, where she stowed it in the backseat. Locating her keys in her purse, she inserted the car key into the ignition and turned it.

A cranking sound occurred, but the engine didn't

catch. Frowning, Drew turned the key again, with the same result.

Her car *always* started, and it had been running perfectly last night. She tried the key again, and then again. Perplexed, she pulled the hood lever and got out. Propping the hood up, she scanned the engine.

Then she felt as if her blood had just been deep-frozen. The coil wire was missing! Nick—it had to be Nick!—had removed the wire from the coil to the distributor cap!

Drew looked around wildly, as though the wire would be lying someplace in plain sight. She took a deep breath, telling herself to calm down, although if Nick were within reaching distance, she would strangle him with intense relish.

Of all the dirty tricks! No wonder he'd left such a casual note. He'd known darned well she'd be here when he got back "around noon," the snake!

It was nearly one when Nick returned. He parked behind Drew's car again and climbed out, looking around with just a tiny knot of uncertainty in his gut. There was a chance she hadn't tried to leave, but that idea was vanquished when he saw the duffel bag in the backseat of her car and the hood up.

He walked into the house, heard nothing and proceeded to the kitchen. Still nothing. He went to the back door and saw Drew. She was sitting on a chair, teetering on its back legs, with her feet on the porch railing. A pair of binoculars were in her lap.

"Hi. The fire's almost out."

She threw him a brief cold glance. "I've been watching it through the binoculars. Aren't you getting a little tired of games?"

"Is this a game to you?" He moved to the railing and leaned against it, a mere few inches from her feet.

Her eyes flashed. "I'm not the one stealing coil wires! Where is it?"

"It's safe. I'll put it back after we talk."

"Fine! What do you want to talk about?"

"What do you think I want to talk about? Us, you and me."

Her eyes were as cold as ice. "Let's start with why you won't leave me alone, when that's exactly what you wanted the morning after we slept together out here."

He studied her. "We'll get to that, but I'd rather start with why you brought me out here that day."

"Well, by all means, if that's what *you* want, let's talk about that!" Drew slammed the front legs of the chair down to the floor and got to her feet, barely catching the binoculars from falling at the last moment. Setting them on the chair, she shot Nick a venomous look. "I had the stupid idea that you might listen to me better out here than in town. Of course, that was before I knew what a heavy-handed jerk you were!"

Nick ignored the insult. "Listen to you about what?"

Drew waved an angry hand. "About the ranch, what else? I didn't want Judd and Simon selling it to a developer. I didn't want this place torn up with roads and destroyed by greenhorns."

"They mentioned something about you being against the sale."

"I wasn't against the sale! I just didn't want you or anyone else ripping this place into little pieces."

"Why didn't you just come to my office and talk about it?"

Drew's lips thinned grimly. "I told you it was a stupid idea. Okay, that's out of the way. Will you give me the coil wire now?"

"What if I told you I wasn't going to develop the whole ranch?"

Drew's eyes narrowed suspiciously. "Meaning what?"

Nick turned to face the view. "I like it out here. I'm having three hundred acres right around the house surveyed out of the projected sales program. There won't be any roads in the immediate vicinity. This part of the ranch will stay just as it is."

He looked at her, because she hadn't said anything. "Does that meet with your approval?"

"I...yes...that's great. It's very...surprising." She was so stunned, her lips felt numb.

"I guess your plan worked," Nick said quietly. "You wanted me to see the place through your eyes, and I did. I found something important up here, Drew." He paused. "You're a big part of it."

Her breath caught. "No...I'm not a part of anything. The place is yours now. I only came this weekend to say goodbye."

"Don't say goodbye," he said softly, and took a step toward her.

She backed up with panic darting across her face. "Don't, Nick. Please."

He held up his hands. "Don't be so jumpy. All I'm asking is for you to stay and talk to me."

"Do I have a choice?"

He hesitated. "Maybe you can't drive off, but no one can force you to talk."

She couldn't answer. What, really, was he asking for? She didn't mind talking, if he didn't try to talk her into something. Into bed again, for example. That was over, even if she did feel him in every cell of her body. Even if when she looked at him, she remembered things she'd rather not, like how he tasted, and how he felt wrapped around her. How it felt to be under him, kissing him, moving with him.

"I'll talk, if you promise to keep your distance," she finally conceded unevenly.

He shaped a small smile. "That's a tough request, honey. It's been over a week..."

"It's going to be a lot longer," she interjected. "Do you want to know what my choices really are? I've been thinking about moving away from Laramie to avoid you. I even talked to my supervisor about a transfer."

His smile vanished. "Do you really hate me that much?"

"Hate" was such a strong word, although the Lord knew she'd thought of it often enough. But she'd also thought about love. Right now she was closer to feeling love than hate, she realized. Nick's aura was influencing her again, no matter how spitting mad she'd been when he showed up.

But she had to stop thinking in extremes. Either loving or hating Nick was wasted energy. What was past was past, which was the one major point she had to get across to him. That and the fact that their affair was not going to taint the future, too.

"I don't hate you," she said wearily. "And I'm not going to leave Laramie, either. But you and I are through. Completely avoiding each other is probably impossible. My family likes you, so if you do any socializing with Judd or Simon we're bound to run into each other. That's fine, but anything else is out."

"I told Judd about us."

Her eyes widened. "You what?"

"He knows I'm here with you."

"Does he know you spent last night here?"

Nick nodded. "Yes."

"Oh, damn," Drew groaned. "I'll never hear the end of that!"

"All we did was sleep. In separate beds, in case you've forgotten."

"Did you tell Judd that?"

"Nope. Must have slipped my mind."

"You deliberately let him think..." Drew's jaw clenched. "Maybe I do hate you. How could you do this to me? Judd still thinks I'm fifteen years old—Simon, too. They questioned me about the three days we were here before. Now they'll drive me crazy with questions and innuendo! You didn't have to say anything to my own brothers. Have you no conscience, at all? Doesn't it..."

Nick threw up his hands. "Would you please shut up!" Drew's mouth hung open, but her tirade had fizzled out. "That's better," Nick said calmly. "Haven't you figured it out yet? No, I can see you haven't. Ask yourself this, Drew. Why would a man confess spending a night with a woman to her brothers? Why would he deliberately omit the fact that they had slept in separate rooms? Why would he chase her until they were both tired of it, and why would he send her flowers for a week, when what he really wanted to do was haul her off to bed and knew damned well he could convince her to go?"

Drew's blood was roaring in her ears. What was he saying? What did he want her to conclude from that confusing barrage of questions? Surely he didn't mean...

Nick moved closer to her. "Don't you know I love you?" he said softly. "I've asked myself when it began. We started out badly. I had so many things on my mind, and so much to overcome. But through it all, I kept thinking about you. You were everywhere I looked, the only thing I saw.

"Drew, you're the toughest woman I've ever known. You never once met me halfway. You fought me in every effort to make amends. You never let me talk, *you* never talked. The only place we communicated was in bed, and even then the communication was limited to sex.

"But that's where you couldn't shut me out." Drew was standing as stiff as a board, staring at him with wide, startled eyes. Nick put a hand on her arm and slowly slid it up to her shoulder. "I think you love me, too, and if you're half the woman I believe you are, you'll forget about the past, once and for all, and admit it."

Thirteen

It was a tremendous amount to take in. Nick loved her? Drew's mind immediately put up barriers of disbelief and stumbled over old hurts.

She dampened her lips and cleared her throat.

"Say something," he prodded gently.

"I...I'm trying."

"Can you say yes?"

"Say 'yes' to what?"

"I'm thinking about getting married."

"You and me? But..."

He put a finger on her lips. "No buts. Either you love me or you don't." He grinned. "It's sort of like being pregnant. Remember what you said? 'It's not a matter of maybe she is or maybe she isn't, Nick.' Well, that's the case with us, Drew. I love you, and if you love me, too, it's off with the old and on with the new for us."

He kissed the top of her head, and then lazily moved his lips to her ear. "Say 'Go for it, Nick' so we can make some plans," he whispered. "I'm aching for you, honey. Tell me you love me."

Drew closed her eyes. She wanted to believe him, desperately, she realized. But this was such an enormous reversal of their stormy relationship.

"I don't...hate you," she whispered tremulously.

He laughed, low and deep in his chest. "And you love my..." He laughed again. "...to make love with me."

She laughed shakily, understanding what he *hadn't* said. "Yes," she whispered.

His hands smoothed down her back, cupping her behind and bringing her closer. "Love me, honey," he urged huskily. "Don't be afraid."

Afraid. Yes, that was it. He'd hurt her so deeply before, and she was afraid she might not forget.

But she did love him. She had loved him all along.

Her hands rose to his chest and she looked into his eyes. "I love you," she admitted softly.

"Will you marry me?"

Tears blurred her vision. "Yes."

He scooped her into a fierce embrace. "Oh, baby, I was so scared you wouldn't be able to say it."

Drew melted into him, but tears remained in her eyes. He was the only man she had ever loved, but there was a small point of hurting in her body that wouldn't relent. Maybe it never would, not completely. But she had made her choice, to marry the man she loved, and the thought aroused some awe. She would have her babies because Nick liked children, and within his embrace, she didn't doubt that he loved her.

He tipped her head back and kissed her lips, lightly

at first, then with yearning. His tongue slipped between her lips and into her mouth, and his hands caressed her bottom. As always with Nick, Drew was losing grasp of everything but the heat he kindled in her body.

"Oh, I do love you," she whispered raggedly. It was such a relief to say it, to stop holding back and just let her feelings flow.

"Oh, I do want you," he returned teasingly. "But I suppose you know that."

How could she not? The proof was nestled against her abdomen.

His eyes seemed to be dancing with devilment. "We could undress out here and prance naked through the woods."

She laughed. "I suppose we could."

His gaze questioned. "I'm not sure you would do such a thing."

"Would you?"

"With you, I might be capable of anything."

"I might be, too. With you." Admitting love was exquisite freedom for Drew. She'd never experienced the euphoric feeling before, not as she did now with Nick.

"Maybe we'll test our inhibitions," he said, adding "later" in a hoarse tone that told Drew exactly what he preferred doing now. His kiss spelled it out even more, along with the heated caresses of his body against hers. "Maybe we won't get out of bed for the rest of the weekend," he whispered. "Only for a little food and water."

The prospect was sinfully stimulating. His open-mouthed kisses and hot tongue created erotic mind images. She wanted him naked, to touch him, to taste him, and she fumbled with the buttons on his shirt.

Her hands were trembling. He was groping, too, yanking the tails of her blouse from her jeans, and they didn't stop kissing.

"Inside," Nick growled. With an arm around her, he opened the screen door and led her into the house. He stopped next to the refrigerator for a long, inflaming kiss, and then, while they held each other and walked down the hall to the bedroom, Drew undid his belt buckle.

He brought her to his room and Drew was astonished to see a king-sized bed. "When did you...?"

"The other one was too small. Com'ere."

He began undressing her. "You're serious about keeping the house and three-hundred acres?" she managed to get out.

"Very. I'm glad you approve. I didn't know how you'd feel about it." Her blouse was tossed to a chair, and he quickly unhooked the back of her bra and slid its straps down her arms. "You're beautiful. Oh, damn, you're beautiful!" Bending over, his mouth opened around a nipple.

Her fingers twisted in his hair. "Oh, Nick..."

His head lifted. His eyes were dark and stormy. "You've turned me into a hungry man. Let's get out of these clothes."

He was magnificently aroused, she saw, as they discarded clothing. Naked first, Drew threw back the blankets and lay down. In seconds, Nick was beside her, pulling her on top of himself. His hands traveled her back, clear down to the sensitive skin behind her knees and upward again.

"I wanted you right away," he whispered thickly. "Right from the first."

Drew raised her head to see his face. "That's not true. You wanted to strangle me."

He grinned. "That, too. But your behind set off bells in my head the first time I got a look at it."

She smiled indulgently. "I heard a few bells, too. You're a good-looking man. I noticed, don't think I didn't."

He squeezed her into a tight hug. "We're going to have a good life, Drew."

"Yes," she murmured, ignoring the little jab of memory that seemed determined to undermine her happiness. It had to be forgotten, to be buried so deeply it never, ever surfaced.

Her kisses moved over his face, finally settling on his mouth. She touched his lips with her tongue, and nestled deeper into the masculine vee of his thighs. The adjustment in their positions aligned everything perfectly, and she seductively rubbed her body against his.

The rubbing and kissing went on until they were both gasping for air. Then Nick rose up and tipped her over. "This way, this time," he said in a passion-roughened voice, intimating to Drew that before the weekend was over, they would make love in any number of positions.

The knowledge was drugging. Being in love and able to say so was drugging. She felt his penetration with some surprise, though, because he wasn't wearing a condom.

It didn't matter. They both wanted babies, and if she went to the altar already pregnant, it would only add to their joy.

"Oh, honey," Nick whispered against her lips. He was moving steadily, a thrusting, masterful rhythm that was making Drew ache with desire. Their overwhelming physical attraction had brought them together, and it would be the indestructible foundation of their marriage.

The little sounds in the back of her throat were raising Nick's blood pressure. She was so exciting, so incredibly hot and perfect for him, as though their bodies had been designed to fit together.

He waited for the signs, for the whimpers, for the clutching of his back and the restless bucking beneath him, constraining the violent release in his own body until she was ready for hers.

It came in waves, in rocketing spasms of mind-numbing pleasure, even more staggering today than it had ever been between them. Drew cried out, again and again, her voice getting weaker with each effort, until she was merely breathing hard.

As was Nick. He put his head on the pillow beside hers and closed his eyes, and they lay there without moving or speaking for a timeless span.

Drew finally kissed the side of his neck. "Are you sleeping?"

Nick raised his head and grinned. "Am I getting heavy?"

"Heavens, no. What ever would give you that idea?"

"Such a sassy woman." Laughing, Nick rolled to the bed. Drew slipped away to the bathroom, snagging Nick's shirt on the way, and, contentedly, he stacked the pillows and lay back with an arm crooked beneath his head. Everything was perfect, exactly as he'd hoped.

Actually, he'd been a little afraid to hope for so much. He closed his eyes and listened to Drew moving around in the house. He liked the sound of a woman's movements.

He was unbelievably happy.

And his stomach wasn't burning in the slightest.

Clad in Nick's shirt, Drew walked slowly into his bedroom. His eyes were shut. The top sheet was draped over his hips and legs. He looked completely at peace and utterly beautiful with his tousled black hair and dark skin. She stood just inside the doorway and gazed at the man she loved to distraction and would marry.

And she remembered the morning when he had turned his back on her.

She winced and clenched her teeth, frightened by the unwanted excursion into the past. Some rebellious part of her was clinging to that wound, but why? No relationship could withstand gnawing resentment in one of its partners. Eventually it would rear its ugly head, in some shape or form, and when it did...?

Drew chewed on her bottom lip. She'd had trouble talking to Nick ever since her first attempt at honesty with him, when he'd become so angry because she had brought him to the ranch without his knowledge. It was odd. With everyone else she was outspoken, if anything.

Nick's eyelids partially opened and he smiled. "Hi. What are you doing just standing there?"

"I thought you were sleeping."

He folded back the sheet. "Come over here and let me hold you." Drew approached the bed. "Get rid of the shirt, honey."

She released the one button she had fastened and let the garment slide from her shoulders and arms, watching the way Nick's eyes took in every detail. Her skin warmed with a faintly pink flush that ultimately reached her cheeks.

"Ah, you do feel good," Nick sighed as she settled into his waiting arms. He pressed a kiss to her forehead and let his free hand drift up and down her body beneath the sheet. "I read somewhere that indifference was the biggest problem in most marriages. I don't think I could ever be indifferent to you, sweetheart, not in a million years."

"A million years is a long time." Teasingly, Drew let her own hand do some drifting.

"Well, maybe a thousand years is a little more realistic."

"Undoubtedly." Her fingers crept into the soft hair at the apex of his thighs. Something else was soft, too, but the second she touched it, it began to change.

"Undoubtedly," Nick echoed with a noticeable cracking in his voice. "You're proving my point extremely well, you know."

"No indifference down here," she quipped.

"None here, either," he responded as he caressed her breast and felt the nipple peak and harden. His mouth found hers, and after a tender kiss he lovingly stared into her eyes. "I've never been happier, Drew."

She hesitated. "You don't have to say that, Nick. I mean, I'm sure you were happy with your first marriage."

His expression sobered. "Do you want to talk about it? I will, you know. If you have any questions or doubts about my past, I'll be glad to discuss them."

"No...of course not," she whispered, ashamed that she had even brought it up.

"You are curious, though, aren't you? I can tell, honey. Believe me, I don't have any terrible secrets."

Nick frowned. "Well, maybe there is one thing you should know."

"A secret?"

Nick lay back and held her head to his chest. "No, not really a secret. After my wife and daughter died, I did some heavy drinking."

An awful feeling welled in Drew. She was making him remember cruel, terrible things. "Nick, don't. I'm sorry I said anything."

"You have a right to know everything. Yes, I'd say I was happy with my first marriage. Mary and I didn't have a whole lot materially, but we had managed to buy a house, and we had Katie. She was a special little girl, Drew, so bright and pretty. She had long, dark curls and almost black eyes."

Drew was weeping silently. "Please," she whispered. "Don't go on, Nick."

He absently toyed with her hair. "I wouldn't face reality. It was so damned senseless. A kid who didn't even have a license was driving the other car. It really wasn't his fault, either. The road was icy. Both cars went out of control.

"Anyway, I drank to blot it out. I barely remember the funeral. I kept drinking. I lost my job and eventually, everything else, too. It took about a year, but I finally woke up and knew I had to get out of Sheridan."

Drew was frozen with compassion and remorse. She shouldn't have mentioned his marriage. What was wrong with her?

Nick took a deep breath. "That's the story. I haven't touched a drop of liquor in four years. I never will again. An alcoholic stupor isn't the answer, Drew."

She was trying to wipe her eyes without being obvious. "Drew?" He tried to raise her chin. "What's the matter, honey? Are you crying?"

A sob shook her shoulders. "I'm sorry," she whispered brokenly. "It's so horrible. How have you lived with it?"

"Through work," he said quietly. "Look at me, Drew." She lifted her tear-filled eyes to his. "I love you. Until I met you, all I had was my work. When I thought you were pregnant, I began to realize what I was missing. I want kids, Drew. I want you and kids and a real life."

She nodded tearily. "I want that, too."

Nick's eyes slowly narrowed. "But something's bothering you, something we haven't talked about."

"No...no..."

"Drew, for God's sake, don't shut me out. Whatever it is, you can talk to me about it."

But it seemed so silly to her. He loved her. She loved him. They were going to be married.

Nick sat up and pulled her up, too. "This feels serious," he said softly. "Is it?"

Drew dragged the sheet up and tucked it across her breasts and under each arm. She wiped her eyes with the back of her hand. "You'll think I'm an idiot."

He tried to grin. "Honey, I think you're sassy and bold as brass, but I'll never, ever think you're an idiot."

It was eating at her, silly or not. "All right," she agreed. "What happened the night we made love up here?"

Nick leaned back against the headboard. "You haven't let go of the anger, have you?"

"I...want to. Very badly."

He reached out and touched the sheet just below her breasts. "And it's all locked up in there, isn't it?"

Her lower lip quivered. "In my heart? Yes, I guess it is."

"But you love me in spite of it."

"I'll always love you."

"Even if I hurt you again with an honest explanation?"

Her shoulders rose with a sudden, sharply drawn breath. "Do you have an explanation?"

His lips turned up with a faint smile. "I'm not sure. Should we give it a try?"

She nodded slowly.

"All right." His eyes took on circumspection. "I was madder than hell about what you did. Every day is—was—planned to the minute. No more of that, by the way, not for my employees, either. Anyway, the landing could have been the end for both of us, and that infuriated me. Worse, though, believe it or not, was the completely unnecessary interruption of my schedule. I couldn't sit still. There had to be a way out of here, I kept thinking, and every time I looked at you, I wanted to shake you until your teeth rattled."

He peered at her. "Are you sure you want to hear this?"

"I'm sure," she said in a tiny, not-at-all-certain voice.

"Looking back, I think what was happening with me was a subconscious effort to block you out. You were too pretty, too sexy, and concentrating on resentment prevented me from admitting I was interested. Women hadn't been important in a long time, and I couldn't see myself getting mixed up with one who spelled trouble."

Drew stole an unsteady breath. His self-analysis seemed entirely logical. Hadn't she also noticed him, felt him deep inside of herself, and fought the attraction?

"Something else was going on, too," Nick continued. "This place was gradually affecting me. I found myself drinking tea and listening to the rain in the middle of the night, feeling strangely contented. You'd have had to know me before, to understand how contrary contentment was to what I'd been living with."

"I knew you were very...uptight."

"To say the least. Anyway, I realized that one night how miserably I'd been treating you. The next day you disappeared. When it sunk in that you were really gone, I went looking. I thrashed around the woods in every direction, and by the time you showed up, I was just about nuts."

"You were genuinely worried?" Drew said, with some amazement. "I thought you were just throwing your weight around."

"I was worried, believe me."

"I hiked out to Black Creek to check its water level." Drew laid a slightly anxious hand on Nick's arm. "The Hoskins ranch is within hiking distance, Nick, but Black Creek has to be crossed to reach it. With so much rain, the creek was impassable. I didn't tell you about it because I was sure you'd ignore the danger and try it.

"Nick, I'm sorry. I should have told you everything and let you make your own decision, but I was worried, too. You seemed so overly confident, so much like my brothers. You couldn't have known the area well enough to strike out cross-country, but I was sure you would try it."

"Am I like your brothers?"

Drew hesitated, then nodded. "Yes, I think you are."

"Is that bad, honey?"

The question reverberated throughout Drew's system. Was it bad for a man to be strong and self-sufficient? Confident? Could she ever love a man *without* those qualities?

Maybe she hadn't fallen in love before because she hadn't met anyone to compare with her tough, macho brothers.

The concept was brand-new and startling. As irritating as Judd and Simon were at times, she admired their masculine spirit immensely. But she, too, was strong and confident, normally. Nick had made her wonder about her own strength and confidence, but those traits were in the LeBeau family's genes, and she wouldn't change either of her brothers an iota if she were suddenly given the power to do so.

She wouldn't change Nick, either, not by so much as one hair on his head.

"No, it's not bad," she said softly. Something was relenting within her. The knot of tension in her midsection was losing substance, and she wanted it to vanish completely. "You surprised me that afternoon with a fire in the fireplace."

"I don't know why I did that. You were cold and wet, obviously, but maybe I just needed to *do* something. Then you came in wrapped in that blanket and everything sort of went upside-down. You sat next to me, and you…" Nick gave her a lopsided grin "…kept getting prettier by the minute."

He took her hand and brought it under the sheet to

his lap. "This started acting up," he said softly. "Just like it's doing now."

"It" was getting very solid in Drew's hand. She loved the feel of him, the satiny texture, the heat and life against her palm. Her eyes locked with Nick's while she very tenderly caressed him.

He dampened his lips and spoke in a less steady voice. "I don't know what happened. One minute I was telling myself to lay off, to cool down, and the next I was touching you. You came to life in my arms."

"I always will," she whispered.

Nick reached beneath the sheet and took her hand. "This discussion is going to come to a screeching halt with much more of that." He brought her hand to his lips for a kiss to her palm. "You have great hands."

"So do you, which I learned very well in front of the fireplace that afternoon."

"That first time nearly took the top of my head off," Nick said after a brief hesitation. The conversation was approaching dangerous territory, those moments when he'd been so disgusted with himself.

His eyes probed hers. "I despised myself after you left the room. I got dressed and vowed to tell you how I felt the second you returned, even though I knew damned well it would hurt you."

The picture was beginning to blur for Drew. Up until that particular sequence of events, she had understood everything Nick had related. "Why did you despise yourself?" she questioned. "You didn't force me into anything. I was as much at fault as you were."

"No, you weren't," Nick said firmly. "Would you have started things between us? I don't think so."

"I could have said no," she rebutted softly.

"Yes, but..." Nick's eyes narrowed. "Why *didn't* you say no?"

"I couldn't. When you touched me, nothing else seemed to matter."

He nodded. "That's what happened with me the second time. I was all set to talk pretty plainly, and then you started fussing with the buttons on my shirt. All my good intentions went to hell. I could smell you and feel you, and I wanted you again so much I could taste it."

A shiver went up Drew's spine. The wanting had been almost palpable, her own, Nick's. How could either of them have denied it?

"Afterward...in the night," she whispered. "You left my bed."

"I woke up in a sweat. You were sound asleep, and the enormity of what I had done was making me half crazy. I was doing business with your brothers, and..." Nick stopped and moistened his lips "...I knew I didn't love you," he finished in a low, barely discernible voice. "I had made love to you twice, and I didn't love you. It wouldn't have bothered me if I hadn't sensed something from you. You gave everything so freely, as though I were someone special."

Drew turned her face away and bit her lip. "You were."

"I got out of your bed and went to my own. Then I lay there and stared at the ceiling. You had to be told the truth. Letting you go on thinking I was special, when I had only made love to you for my own pleasure, was intolerable. First thing in the morning, I told myself. I dreaded the upcoming scene. I didn't sleep the rest of the night. I was still battling an overload of guilt when Judd and the rest of the crew arrived."

Nick took her chin and turned her face back to him. "I was glad, Drew. Not just for the rescue. Facing you with my feelings would have been the hardest thing I'd ever done. I was glad to walk away from the whole mess that morning."

It was as bad as she had suspected. "You used me," she said huskily.

"I thought so...until I started facing the real truth. I fell hard and fast, Drew, but it had been so long since I'd felt anything for anyone, I couldn't begin to comprehend falling in love." He shaped a small, rather helpless smile. "Especially with a woman who had totally disrupted my life. It took a while to digest it all."

Drew knew how vulnerable she was right now, how easily she could say the wrong thing out of defense. That was her way, the LeBeau way, to defend and protect herself. Getting the last word was important to all of the LeBeaus, which accounted for their many battles.

But this went far beyond the usually trivial spats with her brothers. This was soul deep and crucial. Nick was giving her time to assimilate it, to believe him or turn on him. His eyes were anxious but waiting.

It was all so clear now. He had held nothing back, not even those aspects of the story any woman would be loath to hear. His only crime was in not recognizing his feelings when she had known of hers at once.

There was only one more question to ask. "Why did you tell everyone coming up here was your idea?"

Nick's blue eyes regarded her for several moments. "I'm not sure. It just came out without thinking, I guess. I hadn't planned it, I know. It bothered you, didn't it?"

"Yes. I saw it...as payment for..." She stopped at the shock on his face.

"Don't ever think that!" He clasped her shoulders in rock-hard hands. "I never thought of you that way, never!"

She looked into his eyes and felt the last trace of her anger drain away. All that remained in her heart was love, and the sensation was wonderful. Smiling softly, she touched Nick's mouth. "You've made me very happy today," she whispered. "Thank you."

With obvious relief, he leaned forward and kissed her. "I did so many fool things with you, it's a wonder we ever got together."

"You're a persistent man, thank goodness. A lesser person might have given up."

His gaze warmed. "I love you so much."

"I love you more than I can say."

One corner of his mouth turned up in a devilish grin. "There's a fire at Black Creek, but it isn't over by the Hoskins ranch. It's right here in this bed. Want to try and put it out?"

Drew laughed and threw her arms around his neck. "It's never going to go out, Nick."

"You've got that right, honey. You've sure got that right."

* * * * *

American HEROES
AGAINST ALL ODDS

HARLEQUIN®   *Silhouette®*

Please address questions and book requests to: Harlequin Reader Service U.S.: 3010 Walden Ave.,
P.O. Box 1325, Buffalo, NY 14269 CAN.: P.O. Box 609, Fort Erie, Ont. L2A 5X3

PAHGEN

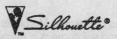

⬤ INTIMATE MOMENTS®
Silhouette®

If you've got the time...
We've got the
INTIMATE MOMENTS

Passion. Suspense. Desire. Drama.
Enter a world that's larger than life,
where men and women overcome life's
greatest odds for the ultimate prize: love.
Nonstop excitement is closer than you
think...in Silhouette Intimate Moments!

⬤ *Silhouette®*

SIMGEN99

FOUR UNIQUE SERIES
FOR EVERY WOMAN YOU ARE...

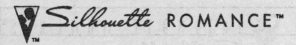

These entertaining, tender and involving love stories
celebrate the spirit of pure romance.

Desire features strong heroes and spirited heroines
who come together in a highly passionate,
emotionally powerful and always provocative read.

Silhouette®SPECIAL EDITION®

For every woman who dreams of life, love and family,
these are the romances in which she makes
her dreams come true.

Dive into the pages of Intimate Moments and experience
adventure and excitement in these complex
and dramatic romances.

Visit us at www.eHarlequin.com   SGEN00

❤ *Silhouette* ROMANCE™

What's a single dad to do when he needs a wife by next Thursday?

Who's a confirmed bachelor to call when he finds a baby on his doorstep?

How does a plain Jane in love with her gorgeous boss get him to notice her?

From classic love stories to romantic comedies to emotional heart tuggers, **Silhouette Romance** offers six irresistible novels every month by some of your favorite authors!

Come experience compelling stories by beloved bestsellers **Diana Palmer, Stella Bagwell, Sandra Steffen, Susan Meier** and **Marie Ferrarella,** to name just a few—and more authors sure to become favorites as well!!

Silhouette Romance—always emotional, always enjoyable, always about love!

SRGEN99R

Silhouette —

where love comes alive—online...

your romantic
life

➤ Talk to Dr. Romance, find a romantic recipe, or send a virtual hint to the love of your life. You'll find great articles and advice on romantic issues that are close to your heart.

your romantic
books

➤ Visit our _Author's Alcove_ and try your hand in the Writing Round Robin—contribute a chapter to an online book in the making.

➤ Enter the _Reading Room_ for an interactive novel—help determine the fate of a story being created now by one of your favorite authors.

➤ Drop into _Books & More!_ for the latest releases—read an excerpt, write a review and find this month's Silhouette top sellers.

your romantic
escapes

➤ Escape into romantic movies at _Reel Love_, learn what the stars have in store for you with _Lovescopes_, treat yourself to our _Indulgences Guides_ and get away to the latest romantic hot spots in _Romantic Travel_.

All this and more available at
www.eHarlequin.com
on Women.com Networks

SECHAN1